To Oli, and Claire

Best regar

Simon

THE HARBOUR MASTER'S SECRET

Simon Thomas

First published 2025
by Rowanvale Books Ltd
The Gate
Keppoch Street
Roath
Cardiff
CF24 3JW
www.rowanvalebooks.com

A CIP catalogue record for this book is available from the British Library.
ISBN: 978-1-83584-104-4
eBook ISBN: 978-1-83584-105-1

Contents

Chapter I:
1921 (Jacques, aged 6)

The heavy air of Léopoldville clung to each member of the Dumont family like a damp cloak as they disembarked from the train, the locomotive's steam hissing behind them as if eager to escape the oppressive equatorial heat. Henri Dumont's boots hit the platform first; his stature cast a long shadow that seemed to slice through the sticky atmosphere of the mighty Belgian Congo.

It was a stifling June afternoon and the Dumont family had mercifully reached their final destination after an arduous two-week journey, mostly by sea, culminating in a day's train ride from Matadi port. Sylvie, with Marie's small hand clasped in hers, stepped down next, followed closely by Jacques, whose youthful eyes were wide with both trepidation and curiosity.

"Stay close," Henri murmured, his gaze sweeping over the throng of people. Porters darted between travellers like shadows, their dark skin a stark contrast to the crisp white linen of European expatriates who paraded around with an air of entitlement.

"*Bonjour*, Monsieur Dumont!"

A lean Congolese porter, muscles rippling beneath his sweat-soaked shirt, approached with a deferential nod. He reached for their luggage, his movements efficient, masking the weariness in his eyes.

"*Merci*," Henri replied, his kindness evident even in this simple exchange. As they made their way through the bustling station, the apartheid nature of Léopoldville revealed itself in the architecture and the rigid lines of segregation – white settlers on one side, Congolese on the other. The cordon sanitaire sliced through the rudimentary city's heart like a scar.

Sylvie clutched at her two children, her discomfort palpable as she observed the disparity around them. Jacques, on the other hand, seemed bewildered, his gaze drawn to the vibrant colours of the nearby market with familiar yet strange items for sale, the scent of spice and smoke, the cacophony of crowds of people communicating in jumbled accents, all intermingling in the sultry air.

The handcart stacked full of their possessions trundled precariously ahead of them, hauled by two strong Congolese porters. The Dumonts, following by horse and carriage, stared silently out at the red sand streets thronging with crowds: young children playing, women casually carrying bundles of long wooden sticks to market balanced on their heads, huddles of men laughing and scheming, rubbish and squalor carpeting much of the ground.

Before long, the dusty, pale municipal buildings that passed for banks, shops, a town hall and a station slipped from view, replaced by more traditional African dwellings – smooth mud-brick walls complete with roofs of thick, tinder-dry foliage. Cheap to erect and even cheaper to fix, if a little susceptible to the heavy monsoon rains, November through April.

Their family procession came to an abrupt halt.

"Papa," Jacques said as he tugged at Henri's sleeve, his blue eyes wide with unspoken questions as he watched the procession of broken men shackled not by chains, but by an invisible yoke of servitude. The labourers, a snaking procession of faces from Africa, China and the Caribbean, were being herded like cattle towards the distant gaping maw of the jungle that threatened to swallow them whole.

The men passing closest to the carriage looked in the windows and met the eyes of its occupants with nothing but despair.

"Look away, *mon fils*," Henri murmured, steering his son's gaze back to meet his own. He could feel the weight of his role here, the silent complicity demanded by his employers. His hands, calloused from years of construction, clenched into fists at his sides; these were the same hands that would now oversee the expansion of colonial greed, lubricated by the blood and sweat of forced labour.

The Dumonts returned in silence to the jolt of their carriage, until eventually the children could make out white picket fences and grass, surrounding clusters of painted wooden cottages. Sylvie and Henri exchanged uneasy glances – the manicured grass, the handful of motor cars, the tree-lined boulevards shading modern homes and shops – it all seemed jarringly discordant with the visceral reality of the mighty Congo, much like a barnacle on a whale.

Nestling in the mzungu, or "white" suburb, their neighbourhood exuded the same mocking elegance as the majority of its European inhabitants. It backed onto fields that whispered secrets of the wild, untamed jungle just beyond. Henri's employer, the Société Nationale des Chemins de fer du Congo, had ensured that their new senior railroad engineer was well-compensated. It seemed more than adequate to the Dumont children, who had been used to the confines of a municipal life and now had all the playground they could wish for.

"Pleasant enough, isn't it?" Henri remarked, though the question carried an undercurrent of sorrow rather than pride that Belgians had forced their way onto this huge land.

"*Oui*," Sylvie agreed, trying to reassure him. Although, deep down inside, she already felt uneasy about meeting the expectations and etiquette of her white European neighbours.

The house was spacious, adorned with all the trappings of European comfort; lace curtains fluttered lazily at the windows, and polished but well-used mahogany furniture reflected the flickering light of two candelabras. Yet the grandeur felt hollow.

In the privacy of their new abode the walls echoed with the silent agreement to shield their children from the harsh truths while wrestling with the guilt of their own complicity. They would take their time ... but each wondered if they could ever come to terms with being an unwelcome settler in someone else's country as easily as their neighbours clearly had.

Right now, morals would have to wait, for they could not rail against the machine without risking everything. The sight of the Congolese porters retreating into the dusky night, backs bent and spirits eroded, was an image that haunted Henri's dreams that first night in Africa.

"Will we be happy here, Papa?" Jacques asked, his voice cutting through the twilight haze.

Henri knelt before his son, placing a firm hand on the boy's shoulder. "We will find happiness together, *mon fils*. And we will remember that every human heart beats the same, no matter the colour of the skin that encases it."

Exhausted and hot, the Dumonts flopped into their beds — the children briefly entertained by the novelty of their mosquito nets — and Marie soon drifted off to sleep imagining she was a princess.

Laying his head on the pillow, Henri Dumont prayed that their time in Belgian Congo would be profitable and safe. *And tomorrow*, he vowed silently to the stars peeking through his window, *I will not look away.*

Chapter 2:
1941 (Jacques, aged 26)

The warmth of the African sun bathing his skin and the feel of dry grass brushing his fingertips evaporated as the raucous cacophony of drunken voices woke Jacques with a jolt. Harsh German punctuated the stillness of pre-dawn and the sun was refusing to rise over Europe. Inebriated tuneless bellowing now clawed at his window, praising the Führer and mocking invisible Jews.

He lay motionless, willing the vestige of warmth from his dream to linger, but the cold reality of Ostend under Nazi occupation was persistent. The oppressive aura seeped through the thin walls, suffocating any remnants of peace.

With a reluctant sigh, Jacques prised his limbs from beneath the warm sheets, the room dimly lit by the meagre glow of a street lamp filtering through curtains worn thin. He moved with mechanical precision, his hands reaching for the starched white baker's uniform hanging stiffly from the back of a chair. His daily armour against the world outside – a world that reminded him of man's innate thirst for domination.

As he buttoned up the uniform his fingers grazed the fabric, each press a reminder of the methodical dedication that had defined his life since the war began. Yet, beneath the routine, something fierce simmered.

His gaze fell upon a small framed photograph perched on the bedside table, the colours faded by time and touch. A young Congolese woman cradling a baby in her arms; both of them etched into his soul. "*Nakupenda sana*. I love you so much," he whispered, gently pressing his lips to the glass. For a fleeting second, he allowed himself to feel the pain again.

Jacques slipped into his polished shoes and pulled a peaked cloth cap over his head before casting a vigilant eye around the modest room. Ensuring nothing was amiss, he fetched his well-worn leather satchel, checking its contents twice. Papers, identity card and the most convincing of all: the purchase order billet, embossed with a swastika, to supply Ostend's highest-ranking German officers with their daily bread – each item was a lifeline, a necessity for navigating the perilous streets before curfew's end.

The bicycle leaned against the wall near the door, its frame cold to the touch as he wheeled it out onto the cobblestones. The 5 am air nipped at his cheeks, a sharp contrast to the oppressive heat that used to drench him in sweat back in the Congo. He mounted the bike, the metal creaking under his weight; a sound that seemed far too loud in the quiet that had finally reclaimed the street.

With one last glance back at his apartment building, Jacques set off into the dim light of morning. His muscles tensed with the readiness of a man who knew the risks that lay ahead; his heart pounded with the resolve of one who had no choice but to face them head-on. The bakery awaited, and with it, the fragile façade of normality he had to maintain.

Pedalling towards the bakery, a familiar sensation stirred within: to make Goliath pay. Sitting by and letting the bullies win again was not an option. Jacques' knuckles turned white on the handlebars, and whilst his empty belly gurgled for breakfast, he knew the real hunger was for vengeance.

The oven's heat blasted Jacques' face as another batch of loaves slid into its fiery mouth. The aroma of baking bread mingled with hints of yeast and flour was a scent that momentarily transported him to a far-off land where dawn broke over the Congo. His hands, caked in white dust, moved with practised ease as they kneaded the dough – a rhythmic dance learned under the tutelage of Maman Nzeza, whose wrinkled fingers once guided his own through the same motions.

Glistening beads of sweat pearled on Jacques' brow, not unlike those he'd shed beneath the equatorial sun. Each press and fold of the dough drew forth memories: the sound of laughter from village children; the rustle of banana leaves in the breeze; the crackling of a wood fire; the first mapa loaves of the day baked in a rudimentary clay oven. Here, amidst the comparative modernity of his Ostend bakery, Jacques allowed himself the fleeting indulgence of these fond memories before reality slapped him back to the present.

The supply of decent ingredients was sporadic, but fortunately Jacques' black-market network was only surpassed by his skill in blending the right amount of filling agent to bulk out the bread, so that it still actually tasted like bread.

By mid-morning, Jacques was threading his way through the streets of Ostend, bicycle laden with the day's wares. He navigated the occupied city with nonchalant ease – leaning into the bends and junctions as if rider and machine shared the same mind, such was the familiarity of his hometown. At each stop, flashing a smile, exchanging pleasantries, showing deference to the grey military men and machines, and making mental notes of every person. German soldiers lounged outside their billets, barking coarse laughter as they tore into the bread marked with the twisted emblem of their Reich – a symbol Jacques baked with calculated precision, ensuring the lines were sharp and the angles true.

"Für sie, meine herren," he'd say, relishing the flicker of surprise as the officers noted his flawless German. They welcomed the flattery, ignorant of the fact that every interaction was a veiled reconnaissance; every compliment a cipher.

With each delivery Jacques collected scraps of conversation, piecing together a mosaic of intelligence – troop movements whispered between mouthfuls, supply shortages grumbled over coffee. This information, seemingly trivial, would later be woven into the fabric of resistance, a pattern only those initiated could discern.

As the morning wore on, Jacques' route took him to hidden corners of the city, where gratitude was silent but eyes spoke loudly. Here, the bread was plain, unadorned by ideology, and handed over with a nod that conveyed understanding. They knew Jacques for who he truly was — a man whose loyalties lay not with the regime that had shackled their town but with the spirit of freedom that refused to be tamed.

Each loaf he placed into outstretched dirty hands was an act of defiance, a subtle rebellion crafted in the glow of an oven's flame and delivered under the guise of daily routine. And though his outward demeanour remained affable and benign, beneath the surface churned a torrent of contempt for the occupiers and a fervent desire to see them undone.

Jacques pedalled on, carried by the same unyielding resolve that had seen him through the humid jungles of his youth. In these streets, amidst the clatter of military machines and the shadow of the swastika, Jacques Dumont was more than just a baker: he was the quietly beating heart of hope, one loaf at a time.

"*Bonjour*, Madame Bernard," he greeted the usually dour frail widow, his French words wrapped in warmth as he handed her a crusty baguette in exchange for a franc. Her watery eyes mirrored a gratitude that went unspoken; their shared understanding needed no language. "If I was 40 years older, I'd make an honest woman of you," Jacques flirted as he pedalled off. A quarter-smile registered on the wrinkled lips of Madame Bernard, who proceeded to remonstrate against his cheekiness under her breath.

"*Goedemorgen*," he greeted a random passer-by, switching seamlessly to Flemish. Charisma was Jacques' currency, and he spent it generously, his smile a beacon of hope in these dark times.

Standing in the kitchen of the town hall, Jacques held out a bag of loaves.

"*Danke*, Herr Baker," said a gruff voice that demanded attention. Oberleutnant Grüber, his uniform crisp in the morning light, felt only gracious sincerity radiating from Jacques as he handed over the goods. "*Ihre brötchen sind die besten.*"

Jacques nodded graciously, receiving the compliment with feigned humility, whilst handing over a specially baked swastika-emblazoned loaf. The soldier slapped him on the back, a gesture meant to be friendly but that sent a shiver down Jacques' spine. Giving as genuine a smile as he could muster, Jacques quickly exited the kitchen and cycled away, searing the Oberleutnant's name and face into his memory.

The air grew thicker with tension as he approached a narrow street lined with grimy buildings, the façade of each one etched with bullet and shrapnel damage. Jacques' blue eyes, so adept at masking his true feelings, scanned the area. He had been here countless times before, but today, something felt "off".

He arrived at the Goldstein residence, where a mezuzah still clung defiantly to the doorframe. The front door was ajar as Jacques leaned his bike against the front window. Taking their order from the basket, he tentatively pushed open the door and stepped inside.

Suddenly, a screech of viciousness and boots pounding on staircase emanated from inside the home, shattering the silence. Jacques' heart pounded against his ribcage like a caged bird desperate for escape.

"*Raus! Raus!*" The guttural shouts of the SS unit ricocheted off the walls. Jacques tripped backwards through the doorframe, rolling onto the pavement outside, barely avoiding the stampede of SS soldiers noisily dragging the petrified Goldsteins out through their own front door, eyes wide with terror. Bread tumbled around him.

"*Was machen sie hier?*" An officer seized Jacques' arm, wrenching him to his feet with an ironclad grip. Jacques' mind raced, his fluency in German now a lifeline.

"*Verzeihung, ich bin der bäcker,*" he stammered, pointing to the loaves for explanation. "*Ich wusste nicht.*"

"Move aside!" Another soldier pushed him roughly, and Jacques stumbled again, awkwardly hitting the kerb and rolling into the gutter. For a moment, his eyes locked with Mr Goldstein's, a silent vow passing between them.

"Get lost, you fool," the officer spat, dismissing Jacques with a sneer. "There's no way a blond-haired, blue-eyed boy like you belongs in this family of stinking rotten Jews! You're bred from the Aryan genes of the fatherland itself! If you weren't the baker I'd swear you were my stepbrother Hans come to visit me from Hamburg! Now, go!"

Heart hammering, Jacques didn't need to be told twice. He righted his bicycle and fled, not daring to look back until he rounded the corner.

Sweat beaded on his forehead despite the chill in the air; breaths came in short, sharp gasps. This was a close call; far too close. As he pedalled faster, putting distance between himself and the scene of despair, Jacques' thoughts were a whirlwind. Compassion for the Goldsteins wrenched through him, fuelling a hatred he could barely contain. But for now, survival was paramount – for him and for the resistance that quietly simmered beneath the watchful eye of tyranny.

I must do more, he vowed. The encounter with the SS had left its mark: an indelible stain on his conscience. A scowl of anger replaced the morning's pretence of cheerfulness.

The afternoon shadows lengthened across Ostend as Jacques returned to the backyard of his bakery. Stowing his bike and slipping wearily inside, Jacques diligently locked and bolted the door behind him with a soft click. Mundane tasks occupied him for a while, making preparations for another day's baking.

That evening, in the darkest corner of the dimly lit bakery cellar, amidst the coppery scent of yeast, Jacques heaved away one of five heavy flour sacks to reveal a circular metal grate covering what seemed to be a drain, just large enough for someone to descend into. With calm familiarity he climbed a little way in, replacing the metal cover overhead, and in complete darkness descended the iron rungs embedded in the wall of the hole. Counting ten rungs down into the depths below, Jacques stooped to walk horizontally for another 36 blind paces, bent double in complete blackness, the familiar scent of damp, cold air chilling in his nostrils. Reaching a wooden wall, Jacques tapped the agreed rhythmic knock on the planks before him: three fast, two slow. Moments later, two of those planks were swung aside to reveal the interior of a wardrobe complete with dresses, furs and coats. Jacques' eyes adjusted as he emerged into a fusty room with no windows, but decorated with moderate comfort: a roughly laid carpet, armchairs, and a bar in one corner comprising nothing but a half-bottle of black-market whisky, several glasses and an ashtray. The Narnian-style wardrobe, from whence Jacques had conjured himself, stood in another corner. Four figures were relaxing uneasily in the armchairs, their expressions etched with the same resolve that coursed through Jacques' veins.

"Any news?" The low tone of Jacques' voice barely rose above the sound of his own breath.

The flicker of several candles cast shadows across the room where Jacques and members of the Groupe G – General Sabotage Group of Belgium (Ostend Brigade) – gathered. Their breaths hung in the air, mingling with whispers that danced with urgency. Next to Jacques' mystery wardrobe, a door creaked open, a sliver of light cutting through the gloom before it was promptly extinguished, plunging them back into secrecy.

"Sorry I'm late," a new voice announced, smooth as polished stone. It was Wout De Vries, the latest recruit to their unit of resistance operatives.

"Ah, Wout, just in time," Marcel announced, his words laced with a forced cheerfulness that failed to mask the tension in the room. "Everyone, this is Wout. He's going to help us get the information we need."

Jacques studied the newcomer. Wout's piercing grey eyes swept over the faces encircling him, a half-smile playing on his lips as if he held a secret no one else was privy to. His handshake was firm, too firm, and there was an unsettling precision in the way he moved, as though every gesture was calculated.

"Welcome to the unit," Jacques murmured, but his words were brittle, lacking warmth.

"Thank you," Wout replied, his tone measured. "I understand your concerns. Trust must be earned, after all."

"Indeed," Simone interjected, her eyes narrowing slightly as she regarded Wout.

The Groupe G members trusted Marcel beyond doubt … always immaculately presented in a tailored three-piece suit, and with a string of military honours to his name, his calm wisdom in the face of Nazi oppression was the stable voice of reason they all needed in this shitshow. He was the embodiment of a great leader, and if Marcel vouched for Wout that meant something … and yet …

Their clandestine meeting continued, the discussions weaving from imminent dangers to possible strategies and tactics. Talk of the fragile alliance between the various resistance cells across West Flanders crackled under the weight of differing opinions.

"Brussels thinks we should focus on sabotage," someone from the corner piped up, a note of defiance in his voice.

"Supply lines," another countered. "Hit them where it hurts."

"Information is our most potent weapon," Wout interjected smoothly. "Resorting to violence requires a level of hardware we cannot source right now, and spells execution for anyone who is apprehended. No … we must understand their plans; predict their moves." His gaze held each member in turn, as if daring them to challenge his assertion.

"Easy for you to say," snapped a plump man named Max. "You come waltzing in here with your talk of intelligence, yet none of us knows what you're truly about."

"Enough!" Marcel commanded. "We can't afford these squabbles. The enemy is out there, not in here."

But distrust had already burrowed deep, like rot in the cellar's damp wood. Jacques caught the subtle exchange of wary glances, the stiffening of postures. This wasn't just tension, it was a chasm growing wider by the minute. And at its centre stood Wout, unflinching; his expression unreadable.

"Let's focus," Jacques said, attempting to steer the conversation back on track. "I nearly got caught up in the Goldsteins' abduction today. They're the ninth family to be taken this week … God knows where. We must warn the Jewish quarter. We'll need safe houses, hiding places, routes."

"Too risky," a voice cut in, cold as the concrete foundations they were encased in. "We should conserve our resources – the Germans are hell-bent on wiping them out, so why risk stopping them?"

"Conserving resources won't save lives," Jacques retorted, his voice edged with steel.

"Nor will recklessness," Wout observed quietly, his words slicing through the heated debate like a knife. "There must be balance in our approach."

Marcel nodded. "Agreed. Let's plan carefully. We'll do what we can. Anything is better than betrayal by neutrality, which seems to be our government's strategy right now."

As the group dispersed, leaving behind murmurs of unrest, Jacques felt the seed of suspicion Wout had planted. The newcomer was right – trust had to be earned. And in a world where the shadow of betrayal loomed large, trust was as scarce as daylight in their underground meetings.

After toiling through the early morning, Jacques sauntered through the shop as the sun as it crept into the sky. He unlocked the door at 9 am sharp, and not a moment too soon for the handful of customers who waited shiftily outside. Customers were waiting shiftily outside. "*Bonjour*, Jacques." Each of them muttered a greeting as they entered, eager to get out of the street before a passing German patrol reached them.

"*Bonjour*," Jacques replied to each, with an understanding smile. He studied all his customers' faces, and registered the faintest hints of accent in the voices of those he didn't know, to try and place them.

The shop was busier than usual that morning and takings were up. Jacques didn't know whether it was the sun shining through the window of his bakery, or if he'd turned the ovens up too high. Either way, he began to feel hotter and dizzier as the morning progressed.

At lunchtime, Jacques locked the bakery door and sat on the shop floor, closing his eyes for a moment, allowing the tiled floor to cool him a little. Sweat still beaded on his pounding head and turned to a chill. It wasn't just the heat of the ovens. It was Africa calling.

A familiar shiver racked his body. Jacques lurched to his feet in a futile attempt to reach Doctor Maertens' house three doors down the street. He stumbled, clutching the edge of the counter for support. No, not now. Not again. He couldn't afford to be weak, to be incapacitated. Yet, as he slipped to the floor again, the bakery walls seemed to melt away, replaced by the dense foliage of the jungle.

He was a child again, hiding behind palm fronds, watching as uniformed men marched through his neighbourhood. Their faces were harsh and unyielding, their hands wielding power with the casual indifference of omnipotent gods. He saw the wizened face of Maman Nzeza twisted in sorrow as they took her son away, the same hands that taught him to knead dough now clenching in helpless fury.

Random feverish hallucinations ebbed and flowed in his mind.

"*Mon père!*" The scream tore from his young lips, a plea to the missionary father who believed he had been called by God to "civilise the blacks" through regular beatings.

"Stay quiet, Jacques." His father's voice echoed in the fever dream, a ghostly admonition from the past. "Don't draw attention – bide your time."

Attention – the very thing Jacques courted every day with his covert activities. Was he any different from his father, skirting the edges of the real fight? The thought clawed at him as the fever raged and his body convulsed on the cool tiled floor.

Through the haze of his malaria, Jacques heard the distant echo of boots on street outside, the guttural laughter of soldiers unaware of the suffering they inflicted with every step. And in his heart, a resolve hardened, tempered by the fires of memory and illness. When this fever broke, when his strength returned, there would be no more skirting. He would act, and let the consequences fall where they may.

For now, the bakery's warmth enveloped him; a deceptive cocoon shielding him from the chill of reality. His breath was ragged, each inhale a battle as the fever held him hostage, the chill of the tiles beneath offering a fleeting respite from the heat that seared through his veins. He tried to lift his head, but it fell back heavy and damp against the floor.

"Easy does it, Dumont," came a voice, cool and controlled – a stark contrast to the chaos racking Jacques' body. Wout De Vries loomed over him, his sharp features blurred by Jacques' sweat-streaked vision.

Wout scooped Jacques under the arms and dragged him out to the back room of the bakery and onto a makeshift bed. In the delirium, Jacques noted that the ovens were off, and the room seemed cooler. *Why Wout? Had he seen Jacques through the window? Was it coincidence?* Then everything went black.

***

A glass of water hovered at Jacques' lips; the liquid's promise of relief tainted by the suspicion clouding his fevered mind.

"Drink," De Vries urged compassionately, tilting the glass.

Jacques complied, the refreshing water cascading down his parched throat. He watched through half-lidded eyes as Wout's gaze scanned the room meticulously, always assessing. There was care in his actions, almost a tenderness, but Jacques couldn't shake the disquiet that accompanied his presence.

"Better?" Wout asked, his tone betraying nothing of what lay behind those calculating grey eyes. "Maertens is on his way with drugs for your malaria. Marcel told me about your childhood … quite a life you've led, Dumont."

Jacques raised his eyebrows and nodded an acknowledgement.

Wout nodded, setting down the empty glass with precision before sitting back on his haunches. His suit, impeccable even in these times of war, seemed out of place in the humble bakery that served as Jacques' sanctuary and prison alike.

"Your fever ... it's been two days now," Wout said, his words deliberate. "They say malaria can unlock secrets of the mind; reveal hidden truths."

"Is that what you're after?" Jacques' question slipped out hoarsely, edged with the mistrust that had fermented alongside the illness within him.

A flicker of something unreadable crossed Wout's face before he smiled thinly. "Merely concerned for a comrade," he replied smoothly.

Jacques' mind raced; fragments of memories colliding with the present.

"Compassion is a luxury in wartime." Jacques' own voice sounded distant, laced with bitterness born of experience.

"Indeed," Wout acknowledged. "Speaking of which, I heard you've been looking for certain ... information?"

"You know, Jacques," Wout reminisced, "my past could be quite useful for you ... I was Head of Colonial Administration at the Belgian Foreign Ministry for many years." He set the trap, and waited for it to spring.

Jacques' heart stuttered. Was it the illness or fear that caused such a reaction? He studied Wout, the man who once orchestrated the fates of many under colonial rule, who knew how to manipulate systems and people alike.

"Information that could help *us*?" Jacques feigned collaborative interest.

"No ... information that could help *you*, Jacques," Wout corrected him.

"It seems that Marcel has told you more than he should," Jacques said, hardly able to believe that Wout, whose trust had yet to be earned, was in possession of Jacques' deepest fears.

De Vries' eyes narrowed slightly, the ghost of a smirk tugging at the corner of his mouth. "A past life," he said dismissively. Yet there was pride there too; a dangerous glint that hinted at the power he once wielded.

"Then help me access some of that old power," Jacques implored, his desperation sharpening his words. "For the resistance."

The room was silent save for the laboured sound of Jacques' breathing. Wout stood, dusting off his trousers with a meticulousness that spoke volumes about the man's nature.

"Perhaps," De Vries conceded, his response hanging in the air like a guillotine's blade poised to drop. "But let's not forget – the price of such favours is often steep."

De Vries departed, leaving Jacques to grapple with his chills and doubts. The Ostend baker knew that somewhere along the line, the price of Wout's help would be extortionate. But the stakes were high and he was desperate. Even as his body trembled with fever, his spirit burned with an unquenchable fire – to fight, to resist, to survive and, most importantly, to find her.

Jacques' fingers clawed at the woollen blanket, crumpled and damp with sweat. Each breath was a battle, lungs heaving against the weight of his illness and the burden of impending decisions. His mind, usually so adept at weaving through the intricacies of language and subterfuge, now staggered through muddled thoughts and half-formed strategies.

Reaching for the water on the floor beside him, Jacques knocked back a couple of chloroquine pills. Every kindness in these dark times was a currency, and Wout's sudden generosity bore the telltale mark of someone who would soon call in their debt.

He set the glass down, a decision made. Jacques turned his gaze to the small opaque window, the pane a cold barrier between him and the world he fought to save. And beyond that glass, the secrets he sought, locked away in offices and whispered in hushed tones by administrators who believed themselves untouchable.

Perhaps in the files that Wout could procure lay the answer to a mystery that had haunted Jacques since his departure from the Congo. Trust was a luxury ill-afforded in wartime and Jacques knew the risks. A dangerous game remained, played by the desperate and the foolish. He worked hard not to show it, but sheer desperation was beginning to get the better of him.

As night seeped through the shop window and into the back room, casting it into darkness save for the faintest glow of the street lamps outside, Jacques closed his eyes and prayed for his health to return. In the precarious balance of fear and necessity, he found a semblance of peace – not in knowing what tomorrow would bring, but in making the decision that he must face it, whatever the cost.

Chapter 3:
1930 (Jacques, aged 15)

Jacques Dumont's laughter mingled with raucously jubilant cries as he dodged through the thick foliage of the Congolese jungle, playing a frenetic game of tag with his best friend. The air was dense with humidity, wrapping around them like a warm embrace. The vibrant sun filtered through the leafy canopy above, casting dappled shadows that danced upon their skin.

Jacques, though distinctly different in appearance with his blond hair and piercing blue eyes, moved with a familiarity that belied his oaky European tan. These young men had forged deep-rooted bonds from the shared adversity and joy of the wilderness. Bobi didn't care about skin colour either – and there was something that intrigued him about this mzungu kid. Bobi smiled. It was nearing the end of the school summer holiday and they had spent so much time together. Bobi felt like he and Jacques were practically brothers.

"Over here, Jacques!" Bobi shouted, beckoning him to join the group gathered in a clearing between the jungle and the round thatched roofs of a Congolese village.

There, Jacques witnessed a sight to behold. A cluster of villagers, adorned not in their dirty everyday clothes, but in an array of flamboyant suits and polished shoes, preparing for a parade through Léopoldville. Their attire was a riot of colours, textures and patterns, each ensemble a bold statement of defiance against the culture of their oppressors. As the two boys pointed and observed, Bobi explained that it was the sapeur tradition – where the Congolese people would save their wages to buy items of luxury European fashion and develop their own sense of haute couture, an unspoken declaration of defiance that true elegance and culture were not matters of race, but of spirit.

Jacques watched, entranced by the confidence with which they wore their finery. The sapeurs performed with a joyful swagger, mocking the pretentiousness of the white women who paraded through Leopoldville. He could feel the stirrings of inspiration; a desire to emulate this expression of individuality. Over time, Jacques wanted this spirit for himself – a blend of the sapeuse style and his Belgian roots, marked by well-pressed creases, a smartly coiffeured appearance and a sense of style – the antithesis of the otherwise conservative attire expected of a young mzungu.

"*Pourquoi?*" Jacques' voice cut through the thrumming rhythm of the scene, his question directed at Bobi standing beside him. Although only 15 years of age, Bobi was a product of the traditional and the modern. Disadvantaged though he was, Bobi was blessed with an intelligent, quick mind that outpaced most of the white students in his class. Jacques often jibed that Bobi should stop making everything look so easy. He had not only a brilliant mind but also a strong physique, made complete with the indigenous knowledge passed down from generations before him. These two young men, brothers in all but looks, taught each other the things that school overlooked. From Jacques, Bobi learned the social etiquette of Europeans (ridiculous though it seemed), plus the colloquialisms of the modern French language. And from Bobi, Jacques learned how to thrive in a wilderness that had everything one could need, and more.

Jacques continued ...

"Why do so many have just one hand ...?" He trailed off, unable to finish the sentence, yet gestured towards many of the men and women of the village with stumps in place of their left hands.

Bobi's gaze dropped, the weight of history and suffering pressing down upon his young shoulders. "*Les marchands de caoutchouc*," he murmured, the words carrying a bitterness that belied his years. "The white men punished those who did not meet their rubber harvest quotas – but not the workers, you understand, Jacques – no, the mzungu needed the men with two hands, so they hurt the ones they loved ... they severed hands from the workers' children and wives to make those men work harder."

The horrendous brutality of the Belgian rubber merchants was no secret, but spoken aloud, it became more than an injustice — it became personal. A heavy silence fell between the boys, the playful energy of moments ago replaced now with a raw acknowledgement of the truth that lay beneath the surface of their shared existence.

Jacques' heart clenched; anger simmering beneath his charismatic exterior. As he looked upon his friend, he felt a profound kinship, a shared sorrow for all those fathers and husbands forced to watch their loved ones being savagely mutilated in the name of white colonial wealth. In that moment, his resolve hardened; he would carry this knowledge with him, let it fuel his actions, and perhaps, one day, help him alter the course of the oppressive tide.

That summer, the two boys became inseparable. Jacques and Bobi were in their own world, oblivious to the raised eyebrows and side conversations of the grown-ups around them, who were surprised at the irregularity of seeing a Belgian and a Congolese boy behaving like brothers in the midst of a segregated world.

And so it was that Jacques Dumont, one evening in 1930, learned how to catch crocodiles with his bare hands.

Jacques' heart pounded in his chest as he and Bobi crept through the dense, swampy, leech-riddled underbrush alongside a small tributary of the mighty Congo River. The air was thick with humidity, carrying the pungent scent of wild vegetation. Despite the sweltering heat, a chill of anticipation settled over Jacques' skin.

"Shh," his friend whispered, holding up a hand. They froze, listening to the distant sound of water lapping against a sandy riverbank. The hunter's signal was clear: their prey was nearby.

Jacques' eyes flicked between the tall trees and the murky river, his senses sharpening. His mother had always said that their home, nestled in the Congo's embrace, should be a haven of love. Yet today, the young boy felt the primal instinct of the wild beckoning him to partake in a rite of passage far removed from the warmth of his family abode.

"Ready?" Bobi asked, an edge of excitement lacing his voice.

"Let's do this," Jacques replied, though his throat tightened around the words.

The plan was set. His friend would lure a croc of "manageable" proportions from its sunbathing on the riverbank, whilst Jacques waited on an outstretched tree branch above the river itself, armed only with his courage and a sharpened stick.

Bobi splashed into the water, sending ripples outward. A deathly silence ensued, broken by the sudden thrashing of water as a crocodile, which from nose to tail was as long as the boys were tall, slithered from the muddy bank into the river. The beast surfaced; its predatory gaze locked onto the teenage bait.

Jacques' breath hitched. This was the moment. He steadied his grip, feeling the bark bite into his palms. Upstream, the sleek form of the crocodile cut through the surface, in pursuit of Bobi who was swimming powerfully towards the outstretched bough.

With a burst of adrenaline, Jacques launched himself from the branch, plummeting towards the creature beneath. Time slowed as he aimed for the crocodile's back, his weapon poised. He landed on its gnarled back with a jarring thud, clamping the beast in a headlock with his left arm as he drove the stick down with all his might into the space at the base of its skull.

The crocodile thrashed violently, and Jacques held on as if his life depended on it, but found himself being rolled under the surface. In a heartbeat, Bobi had returned to grab the beast's torso, and with both boys finding their footing on the riverbed, it wasn't long before they had hoisted the croc into the air and were striding through the shallows back to the riverbank. Finally, the majestic creature lay still. Jacques watched in awe and sorrow, as the light faded in the crocodile's eyes, and a strange sense of connection passed between beast and boy.

As they tied up the prey with reeds, ready to transport it back to feed Bobi's family, a crowd of villagers gathered round in admiration. Jacques punched the air in triumph. The shrill ululation of tribal singing could be heard all around in celebration.

"Brave mzungu!" they exclaimed, thronging around Jacques, ruffling his hair and shaking hands vigorously. "One of us!"

As they prepared the feast, Jacques' thoughts drifted to his own parents. They had tried so hard to shield him from the darkness of their times, fostering a nurturing environment amidst chaos. But here, in the heart of the Congo, bravery and initiative had been his true protectors.

That evening, as the village rejoiced with a sumptuous feast and harmonious, mesmeric tribal chanting, Jacques savoured the taste of camaraderie and acceptance. In the fiery glow of the celebratory flames, he realised that home wasn't just where love resided; it was also where you stood your ground and fought for your place in the world.

Around the fire, Bobi translated as the elders shared stories of horrific brutality from their youth. Jacques could scarcely believe how his own people could treat other humans so cruelly. Bobi knew a place where it was still happening, and, not fully believing in the truth of it all, Jacques agreed to follow.

Climbing easily over the fence that carved a straight line through the jungle, the two boys continued their quest for proof with the brightness of a setting sun shining the way.

"Come," whispered Bobi to his friend, an urgency propelling them towards the glow of lights surrounding the rubber plantation compound. Peering through the thick underbrush, they witnessed a scene which would sear itself into their young minds.

Naked Congolese workers stood with mouths full of rags, coated in a glistening sheen of rubber sap, trembling as it dried from their body heat and the warm evening air. Then, without warning, the white plantation manager began his harvest. With a cruel efficiency, he stripped the hardened rubber from their flesh, eliciting muffled screams that cut through the still air like sharpened blades.

"*Mon Dieu*," Jacques gasped, horror constricting his throat. Beside him, Bobi's knuckles whitened with suppressed rage.

"Quiet," Bobi hissed, grabbing his friend's arm. They could not afford to be caught spying on this brutal act of exploitation.

But the two boys had ventured too close to the edge of the compound; their presence now dangerously exposed. A guard's voice crackled through the air, sharp and authoritative.

"Who's there? Show yourself!" The flash of his machete now dangerously close to Jacques' neck.

Panic gripped them both, rooting them to the spot … and then from nowhere, Namiri Mbala emerged from the foliage, wearing the red robe of a village elder, his presence commanding yet calm. Bobi's relief at seeing his uncle Namiri by his side in that moment was palpable. The elder had noticed the boys leaving the village in darkness and knew teenage mischief when he saw it.

"Ah, m'sieur! I was just checking the perimeter and my two boys strayed onto the plantation land – forgive them, they are young," Namiri said smoothly, his voice betraying none of the fear that gripped them all.

The guard squinted into the dim light, suspicious at the village elder referring to a mzungu as "one of my boys". "Why at this hour, Mbala?"

"Leopards, m'sieur. We've seen tracks," Namiri replied, gesturing towards the brush with calculated casualness. "Can't be too careful."

The guard nodded, his attention diverted just long enough for Jacques and Bobi to slip away, their escape covered by the sounds of the jungle night.

Namiri escorted the teenage rebels from the jungle and across the fields in silence, to the relative safety of the Dumont home. They were greeted by Henri, who was poring over technical drawings in the lamplight of the front porch. The weary engineer smiled lovingly at the two boys and hugged his son. Jacques sheepishly introduced his father to Namiri – Bobi's uncle – predicting a severe ticking off. To his amazement it seemed as though the two men were already acquainted. Henri recognised Namiri instantly as one of the railway foremen from the railroad gang. Henri had noted that the labourers had much respect for the powerfully built Congolese elder. Even when working, Namiri carried out his duties with pride and respect. But what was he doing here, at his home?

Henri quickly ushered the three of them inside for some refreshment. After Jacques and Bobi had confessed sheepishly to their misdemeanours, Namiri and Henri offered words of warning to their young men (both boys were relieved not to receive a full-blown punishment for getting themselves into danger). Sylvie, as hospitable as ever, provided tea and sandwiches, leaving the men to reminisce about the misadventures of their own youth. Henri and Namiri built an even deeper respect and friendship that night, and as a mark of gratitude, Henri invited Namiri to bring the Mbala family over for dinner later that week, agreeing to keep the event as secret as possible.

Beside Jacques' bed later that night, Henri noticed a look of devastation on his son's face.

"Father," Jacques asked, "how can such cruelty exist?"

Henri met his son's piercing blue gaze, the same question having haunted him for years now. "I wish I knew, Jacques. But it is our duty to be different, to show kindness where others show none."

***

It wasn't long before the Dumonts welcomed the whole Mbala family quietly into their home, via the back door of the friendly mzungu house, to arouse minimal suspicion from the neighbours.

Under the cloak of darkness, the Dumont residence windows were shuttered against prying eyes. There was some tension as

Sylvie had spent the afternoon preparing for her local guests. She had never welcomed a Congolese family into her home before. It felt right to offer their hospitality to the Mbalas, after Namiri had safely returned Jacques to them. As Sylvie fussed happily over everyone, she couldn't help but peer out nervously through the front door every now and again – gossip spread faster than wildfires in this neighbourhood.

And so there was an air of tension and expectancy as both families began their friendship, in an act of silent rebellion against the colonial order of things.

"Thank you for coming," Henri whispered, his blue eyes earnest in the low candlelight. "I can never repay what you've done for my son."

Namiri simply nodded; the weight of gratitude shared between them heavier than words could convey. The families gathered around a modest table; the clink of china a delicate symphony in the stillness of the night.

"Please, let us have tea," Henri offered, pouring the steaming liquid with a steady hand. "It is not much, but it is with our deepest thanks."

The Mbala family accepted with quiet dignity, the children's eyes wide with a mix of curiosity and apprehension. They were in the house of their father's boss, a world apart from their own, yet here they were treated not as subordinates, but as equals; honoured guests in the dead of night.

As the tea infused the air with its aromatic warmth, so the two families began to enjoy each others' company. The walls of colonialism crumbled, and they found common ground, united by the courage of a Congolese foreman and the compassion of a Belgian engineer.

"Your bravery will not be forgotten, Namiri," Henri stated, his voice barely above a whisper. "In these times, we must look out for one another. Our humanity demands it." (Jacques helped to convey the sentiments in both French and Swahili.)

Namiri met Henri's gaze, a silent acknowledgement passing between them. They understood the risks and potential consequences that loomed outside the safety of this secret gathering. But for now, they savoured the simple joy of camaraderie and cake; the flickering candlelight casting a hopeful glow upon the faces of two families.

From the very moment the Mbalas set foot inside the Dumont home, Jacques felt it. Not the lingering excitement of his recent narrow escape, nor the jeopardy that this illicit gathering represented, but the sight of Ana Mbala as she entered the dimly lit room. To begin with, all he could do was stare and smile ... the way her stunningly beautiful face and braided hair were framed by the soft glow of the candles. He was alert to every movement of her body, walking through from the kitchen to place plates of cassava and spiced fish on the table with such serenity and grace, her dark eyes occasionally meeting his with the electricity of attraction.

The air between them was effervescent; an invisible energy. A silent symphony played out in glances and half-smiles between the two teenagers. Each aware of the gravity of their attraction, they were helpless moths drawn instinctively towards a flame in a world where all of this was forbidden. Neither of them seemed to care what society found unacceptable. From the moment they laid eyes on each other, nothing and no one else mattered.

"Ana," he whispered in Swahili when the opportunity arose for a stolen moment away from the vigilant eyes of their parents. "Your name, it's as beautiful as the evening stars."

She rolled her eyes as if to say, *Oh please ... is that the best chat-up line you've got, mzungu?* "*Non*, Jacques. In our village, the name 'Ana' means 'grace'," she replied, her voice tinged with the melody of her native tongue, plus a little teenage sarcasm for good measure.

"Grace," Jacques echoed, tasting the word as if it were as exotic as the spices that lingered on his lips from dinner. Their conversation was a dance, each word carefully chosen, steps taken around the unsuspecting truth of their growing affection.

"Tell me," Jacques pressed on, driven by his characteristic bravado, "what would you like to do when you leave school?"

Ana paused, considering the risk of revealing too much. Yet there was something in Jacques' earnest gaze that compelled her to open up, to share the visions she harboured for a future untainted by the harshness of colonial rule. They spoke in low tones, exchanging hopes and fears, their words weaving a delicate tapestry of connection. And the more they talked, the longer they gazed into each other's eyes, and the deeper Ana fell for him.

From that moment – helplessly cradling their hearts in each other's hands, everything else melting away, including the harsh reality of their existence – each laugh and each shared secret was an act of defiance against a world that sought to divide them.

As the evening meal drew to a close, with the rest of the gathering completely oblivious to Jacques and Ana becoming totally smitten with each other, Henri and Namiri expressed gratitude and concern. The fathers understood the perils that faced their families, even as they themselves had dared to cross the invisible lines drawn by society.

Jacques lay awake long after the Mbala family had departed, the details of Ana's face, body, voice, scent, all searing his thoughts. In his mind, he replayed their exchange, each word branding itself deeper into his soul. He knew that what was blossoming between them was more than just youthful infatuation. For the very first time, Jacques Dumont was in love.

Amidst the freedom and prison of the Belgian Congo, Jacques made a silent promise. He would fight for her. In Ana's eyes, he saw not only the reflection of his own longing but the promise of a world, somewhere far from here, where they could be together.

***

The new term began later that week at Santa Maria Missionary School. The strict missionary fathers observed segregation as much as possible, but it was impossible to prevent all contact, and Jacques made the most of this loophole. Father Dax eyed him suspiciously as Jacques became the most helpful student in the class, offering to hand out all manner of items from paper to food. Every time, he felt Ana's hand brush against his under the items he distributed to each class member. A jolt of connection surged between them, until Jacques' bliss was violently shattered by the sharp crack of a hard wooden ruler on the back of his knuckles as a preventative measure against observing incorrect segregation with the Congolese pupils. Jacques did not care one bit … a little pain was worth every secret touch.

"Is there something you find more engaging than my lesson, Mr. Dumont?" The missionary teacher's voice dripped with icy contempt as he loomed over Jacques, eyes darting suspiciously between him and Ana.

"No, Father," Jacques murmured, bewildered at the mystical powers of observation shown by the priest to notice his affection for Ana.

"Stand up, both of you!" The command felt like a whip in the stillness of the classroom. Reluctantly, they rose, heads bowed, as the other students watched; a mixture of fear and pity in their eyes.

"Disgraceful," the teacher spat out, circling them like a predator. "The son of a respected engineer and the daughter of a lowly foreman exchanging forbidden affections in my class."

He struck again, this time slapping Ana's face hard. She stifled a cry but the force of the strike sent her to the floor. Jacques' jaw tightened, eyes blazing with fury. To strike out would be disastrous, yet to remain passive was torture.

"Your parents will be informed of this insubordination!" spat Dax. "See me after school, Dumont."

***

"Mr Dumont." The missionary teacher addressed Henri with feigned respect. "I must inform you of your son's inappropriate behaviour with the Mbala girl. It brings shame upon your family and disrespects our Catholic values."

Henri's gaze shifted between the missionary and Jacques' swollen hand. "I will deal with this, *mon père*. May I have a word with my son, now?" he asked, his tone even but firm.

In the school grounds, under the shadow of an ancient baobab tree, the two stood facing each other – father and son, the weight of unsaid words hanging heavy between them.

"Jacques, look at me," Henri urged. Jacques lifted his gaze, revealing tears streaming down both cheeks. With clenched fists he reached out and wrapped both arms around his father's waist, clamping his head to Henri's broad chest, and wept.

"Papa, I—" Jacques started, trying to compose himself, but Henri interrupted.

"I know," Henri said quietly, reading his son's heart like an open book. "Your mother and I, we've seen how you look at Ana. We understand more than you might think."

Jacques' shoulders slumped, relief mingling with apprehension. "What will happen now?"

"Listen to me, Jacques. There are dangers here that you are only beginning to understand," Henri cautioned, his wisdom born of years living among the harsh paradox of colonial Africa. "But I see the Dumont determination in you; the same resolve that brought your mother and me to this land."

"Does that mean—"

"It means," Henri interrupted again, holding Jacques' head gently in both hands and pausing momentarily to wonder how his baby boy had grown up so fast, "that we must tread carefully. I'm trusting you here, son. And I won't stand in your way – love doesn't care about who or where or when, it just happens. But Jacques … it's dangerous to love here … be careful."

"Thank you, Papa," Jacques whispered, the gravity of their situation not lost on him. Together, shoulder to shoulder, they sauntered home chatting about the news of political storms brewing in Europe.

Chapter 4:
1942 (Jacques, aged 27)

The scent of fresh bread wafted through the narrow streets of Ostend, mingling with the briny tang of the North Sea air. Jacques Dumont was beginning to feel better, although his cheeks were still pale from the recent bout of malaria. Adjusting the scarred baker's gloves and wiping perspiration from his brow, Jacques slid another steaming tray from the oven. As golden loaves lined the shelves, it wasn't just the racks of bread that were easier to lift – Jacques' motivation was growing stronger too.

Outside, the town was waking, a deceptive calm settling over the patched concrete and cobblestone roads, punctuated by Nazi checkpoints. Jacques had learned their routines, knew their comings and goings, and understood that even the occupiers could not resist the charm of a well-baked baguette. A moment of clarity – despite his feigned pleasantries and the oppression that surrounded them – that humans craved normality amidst this madness. This was the exchange that

Jacques offered — bread and a smile; a little slice of normality. And with normality, peace.

He scanned the street through the bakery shop window and observed Wout De Vries striding purposefully amongst the morning bustle, his figure, although dressed to blend in with the townsfolk, cutting through the crowd with predatory efficiency. Jacques' pulse quickened in preparation. Today, he would confront Wout ... today, he needed Wout. Jacques sensed that it was like inviting a snake into your home, but he was out of options. It had to be Wout, and it had to be today.

After stepping out from the warmth of his bakery and deftly locking the door behind him, Jacques quickly darted across the street to shadow De Vries, unobtrusively matching his pace and direction. He tailed Wout unseen through bustling streets and a maze of alleys until Jacques found the moment to intercept at a secluded nook behind the old Protestant church, away from prying eyes and ears.

"Wout," Jacques asserted, his voice steady.

Wout turned, his grey eyes narrowing as he registered Jacques' presence. "Dumont," he greeted, his tone cautious. "I didn't expect to see you up and about so soon."

"Neither did I — it must have been the exemplary medical attention I received," Jacques replied, hiding thinly veiled gratitude behind his neutral expression. "And I have another favour to ask. One that requires your particular ... talents."

"Go on," Wout said, folding his arms across his chest, the picture of cool appraisal.

Jacques took a breath, feeling the weight of what he was about to propose. "I need to trace a girl, an orphan — part of the Congolese repatriation project your department managed in Brussels. I need to find her, Wout. And I believe you can access those files."

Wout's gaze held Jacques' for a long moment, the silence between them thick with unspoken calculations. The smugness of satisfaction spread inside Wout's gut as he realised the leverage potential. *What a fool*, he thought. Dumont would pay dearly for his desperation.

Finally, Wout unfolded his arms and let out a slow, deliberate and vaguely dismissive sigh. "You know the risks involved, Jacques. For both of us."

"I do," Jacques said, his jaw set. "But she is important. I have to try. I'll do whatever it takes, De Vries."

A thin smile crept onto Wout's lips; one that didn't quite reach his cold eyes. "Very well," he murmured. "We'll see what can be done. Rendezvous tomorrow night at the docks. Oh … and Dumont … You *owe* me for this."

Jacques watched Wout the snake turn on his heel and slither away, disappearing into the maze of Ostend once more. A wave of relief washed over him, tempered by the knowledge that the path he had just chosen was fraught with danger. Returning to his bakery, Jacques felt the familiar press of dough beneath his fingers, each loaf shaped with the same care and precision that he would need to navigate the treacherous road ahead.

***

Under the guise of night, the two men rendezvoused at a deserted dockside warehouse as planned, with the scent of salt and rust hanging heavy in the air. The only light beamed through skylights from the full moon, casting angular shapes along the cracked walls and dusty floor.

"Your bread has charmed their palates," De Vries began, his voice smooth as he stepped out of the darkness, "but now we need it to open doors ... more specific ones."

Jacques tensed, his senses sharpening. "Go on," he urged, treading cautiously in this conversational minefield.

"High-profile intelligence," Wout continued, his eyes glinting with avarice. "Documents that could change the course of our struggle. You're going to help us steal them."

The blood in Jacques' veins turned to ice. This was not mere espionage; it was a gambit that could cost him his life. Yet the stakes were clear — the location of the girl eluded him, a prize just out of reach.

"Steal? How?" Jacques asked, his voice steady despite the turmoil brewing within.

"Simple," Wout replied, with the kind of smile that was all mouth and no eyes. "Use your bakery runs. Get close to the commanders in the town hall headquarters, closer than you've been. Then, when the time is right, you take what we need."

"And the orphan information?" Jacques pressed, needing to hear the promise.

"Upon successful delivery," Wout assured, though his words felt like a verbal spider's web waiting to entangle. "But let's be clear, Dumont. If you're caught, there's no rescue plan. You'll be on your own."

"Understood," Jacques said, this time bluffing confidence, of which in reality, he had none.

"Good." Wout nodded, satisfaction curling the edges of his lips. "We get what we want, and maybe I get a little recognition for my trouble. Those damned Allies will thank me after the war."

Jacques' jaw clenched, but he held Wout's gaze. This dance with the devil was necessary, for her sake. He would play along, for now. "When do we start?"

"In two days," Wout said, turning his back on Jacques and vanishing into the shadows once more. "Prepare yourself. Soon we change history – or you'll become it."

Standing alone amidst the creaks and groans of the old warehouse, Jacques allowed himself a moment to feel the weight of the proposition. And the darkness reminded him that there was no turning back.

The night air clung to Jacques' skin with a chill that seeped into his bones as he paced the narrow confines of a small, dimly lit room above the bakery. His footsteps were silent, but his mind roared with doubts and fears. The plan laid out before him by Wout was treacherous, beset with hazards that could endanger his life in an instant. Yet the shimmering thread of hope it offered – the chance to find Kamia Dumont, his only daughter – tugged at his heart with relentless urgency.

Jacques stopped at the small, cluttered table that served as his makeshift desk, his hands trembling slightly as they hovered over the worn map of Ostend spread out before him. He traced the route from the bakery to the Nazi headquarters with a finger, each street and alleyway a potential risk. Could he really navigate this labyrinth of danger for the sake of a promise so fragile it might as well have been spun from fog?

He leaned closer to the map, his eyes reflecting the flicker of the lone candle that illuminated his plans. The soft glow cast shadows across his face, deepening the lines of worry that creased his brow. With each breath, he fought the rising tide of panic. A single misstep, one faltering moment, could doom not just himself, but the entire resistance effort, maybe even the lives of innocents caught in the crossfire.

"Kamia," he whispered. Her name brought comfort against the darkness that threatened to engulf him. Mental images of her tiny hands and perfect fingertips, the way her eyes sparkled, her lips smiled … never had a father loved a baby daughter so much. To find her, for just one cuddle, to smell her soft skin again, he would walk through hell. For her, he would risk a firing squad consisting of the entire Wehrmacht.

Welling up with tears, Jacques reached for a sheet of paper and a pen. His hand was steady now, as if the act of decision had calmed the storm within. He composed a brief letter; the words a code known only by a trusted few – a signal of the impending danger, a plea for assistance should everything crumble to ashes. The missive was concise; a mere whisper of ink that carried the weight of his world.

"Trust is a luxury, old friend," Jacques murmured to the empty room as he sealed the envelope. No names marred the surface, only the Brussels address – a destination that might mean salvation or betrayal. He stowed the letter inside his jacket, feeling the press of its edges against his chest like the beat of a second heart, erratic with fear and purpose.

Dawn was a mere suggestion on the horizon as Jacques stepped outside, the bakery's familiar scent a bittersweet farewell. The curfewed streets of Ostend lay hushed, blanketed in the deceptive calm of the early hours. He moved with purpose, his steps a silent prayer, blending into the shadowy night towards the nearest postbox, kissing the letter for good luck before sliding it in.

His task for Groupe G, for Wout's ambition and his own desperate need, loomed ahead; a plan laced with risk. But Jacques Dumont, once a boy who played along the banks of the mighty Congo River, now stood as a man about to dance on the edge of a knife. She was all he had left, and the thought of losing her to this godforsaken war ripped him apart.

"May fortune favour the foolish," he breathed. And with the letter dispatched into the belly of an unreliable postal system, Jacques turned back towards destiny's winding path, ready to play his part in the deadly theatre of war.

***

Next evening, the familiar candles flickered on the walls of the hidden Groupe G meeting place where Jacques Dumont now stood, sipping a whisky to calm his nerves. He was a man whose very existence had become a tightrope walk above an abyss. Safe to say that the words of advice and encouragement uttered by his resistance comrades fell well short of easing Jacques' fears.

"Remember," Wout's voice cut through the silence with surgical precision, "the officers will be distracted only for a few minutes. In and out swiftly. No heroics."

Jacques' blue eyes flickered with a silent promise as he nodded; the weight of what lay ahead settling over him like chain mail. Beneath the stoic masks of Groupe G lay the knowledge that if Jacques were caught, the cherished baker of Ostend would face a fate far worse than any oven's fire; a fate that would likely come knocking for each of them in turn.

"Your charm is your best weapon," Wout continued, his grey eyes locking onto Jacques'. "Use it to move freely among them. But do not forget: these men are our enemies."

Jacques felt his jaw set in response. He thought of the laughter that always greeted his arrival in the Nazi headquarters (which doubled as the town hall when Belgium wasn't being held captive), the casual conversations shared over the scent of fresh bread. Those moments would now be poisoned by deceit, every smile a mask over the grimace of a man with everything to lose.

"Once inside the Commandant's office, photograph whatever documents you find. We need intelligence that will change the game." Wout's words were a knife, carving out Jacques' duty from the block of his trepidation.

"Understood," Jacques responded, his voice steady despite the tremor that threatened to betray his fear. The plan was madness – a ballet danced on the head of a pin – but there was no turning back. For Kamia, for all the silenced voices of the resistance, he would play his part to bring down Goliath.

"Good. The decoy signal will be an explosion outside. When the officers evacuate, it begins." Wout gestured to the door, the meeting drawing to a close with the urgency of their mission pulsing in the air.

Here, in the belly of Ostend, a plan had been forged that might end in celebration or in mourning. With one last look at the faces of his comrades, Jacques turned and resolutely made for the exit.

The bakery awaited, its ovens a familiar haven. But tomorrow, they would serve as the prelude to an act that could either elevate the resistance or crush it under the heel of the Nazi boot. Needing some fresh air to clear his mind, Jacques chose not to return via the wardrobe tunnel, instead stepping out into the breaking dawn. The labyrinth of Ostend stretched before him, unaware that its beloved baker was walking towards a crossroads in history.

Jacques' fingers trembled as he loaded the camera, a weapon of espionage, then carefully nestled it in the inside pocket of his flour-dusted, three-quarter-length black leather delivery jacket. He glanced at the clock on the wall for the hundredth time.

Leaving the bakery at 8.50 am with a delivery bound for the town hall, adrenaline was pumping through him. His legs felt heavy and weak. The vibration of the bike protesting across the lumpy cobbled sections of the road exacerbated the jittery feeling in his arms and the rising sense of nausea.

Propping the bike around the rear in the usual place, Jacques headed inside with the order.

The clock on the front of the town hall struck nine. Two minutes later, he expected a distraction. Two minutes of eternity.

Boom! At 9.02 am exactly a parked car exploded across the street, peppering blast fragments across the front of the town hall, several windows shattering. It sent the Germans into panic … their HQ became a noisy confusion of German officers shouting commands, grabbing weapons and heading outside to defend what they imagined to be some sort of attack.

This was the moment to act.

Nimble and sharp, Jacques navigated the corridors of the old building to the Commandant's office, guided by memory and scent – the acrid musk of leather and decent cigarettes.

The door to the office was ajar, just as planned. He slipped inside, noticing rows of filing cabinets and the large oak desk that dominated the room, a cracked red leather chair swivelling away behind it. There it was, atop the pristine surface: a map splayed open like a fan, its edges weighted down by a glass ashtray on one side and an iron eagle paperweight on the other.

He raised the small camera, framing the map within the viewfinder. His right finger pressed the shutter button and … nothing … silence. Again and again, his finger becoming more agitated as Jacques' breath stalled. A cold dread snaked up his spine as he tried again, only to be greeted with the same eerie quietude. The camera had jammed.

"*Verdammt*," he muttered under his breath, the German curse only adding to the dread in his stomach.

Jacques' mind raced, and a surge of desperation propelled him forward. He couldn't leave empty-handed – not when Kamia's life was at stake. With a precision that belied his panic, he swiftly folded the map, edges creasing in protest, and thrust it out of the open window into the embrace of the grey morning. It was a gamble, one that could cost him dearly if the wrong eyes were drawn to the fluttering paper caught in the morning breeze.

He turned on his heel, the baker re-emerging from within the spy's guise. The corridor was a gauntlet, but Jacques' steps were measured, his expression schooled into the pleasant mask everyone knew – the amiable baker delivering his daily wares.

As he entered the kitchen, the aroma of a bubbling stew wrapped around him like a comforting shroud. The cook, a portly man who sweated profusely at all times of day, glanced up and gave a curt nod.

"Right on time, Jacques," the cook grumbled, unruffled by the commotion enveloping the situation.

"Always," Jacques replied, his voice carrying the warmth of fresh loaves, even as his heart thundered against his chest.

And there they were, the German officers returning from their momentary distraction, their boots echoing ominously along the stone floor. Jacques kept his composure, exchanging pleasantries about the weather and the consistency of today's dough with the cook, as the officers passed by. Their voices, guttural and authoritative, faded into the distance, and for a fleeting second Jacques allowed himself the hope that his ruse had succeeded.

He prayed that it would be some time before they discovered the missing map. Until then, Jacques was still the beloved baker, his secret mission concealed beneath a veneer of flour and yeast. But he knew all too well the clock was ticking, and every moment he delayed was another step closer to capture.

As he slipped through the back door, the heavy air of the kitchen gave way to the sharp bite of the autumn breeze. Jacques didn't allow himself to hesitate, knowing that each second squandered could seal his fate. His mind raced with the potential consequences of his actions, but his limbs moved with singular purpose.

Rounding the corner of the stately building, his polished brogues slipped across the damp grass. The bushes loomed ahead, a tangle of shadows beneath the office window. Jacques dropped to his knees, his hands probing the foliage with frantic urgency until they closed around the crumpled edges of the map. Withdrawing it like a precious relic, he tucked it securely into the inner pocket of his coat, its presence burning against his chest.

Before he could rise, a cacophony erupted from within the building. Shouts in harsh German pierced the stillness, followed by the unmistakable sound of booted feet thundering down corridors. Jacques' breath caught in his throat; the map's absence had been discovered already.

From his crouching position, he glimpsed uniformed figures swarming the grounds, their movements chaotic yet purposeful. Orders were barked out, and the search parties began to fan out like hounds on the scent. Jacques knew they would soon scour every inch of the compound. His identity as the affable baker would not protect him if they found the map on him.

He scanned the perimeter, every nerve alight. Time was slipping through his fingers, and with it, his chance at freedom. He mustered all his wits, the cunning that had always been his ally, and made a split-second decision. There was no going back — only through the intricacy of Ostend's streets could he hope to evade capture.

With the agility of desperation, Jacques rose and darted along the side of the building, away from the growing commotion. He headed for the security of people. Jacques entered the winkelcentrum, the maze of shopping streets, with its stream of shoppers, and slowed to a walk, matching their speed and mannerisms, the map his damning secret, his steps light but laden with the weight of what he had set into motion. He was the thief, the saboteur — the man who had dared to steal from under the noses of the enemy. And now, the hunt was on, an abandoned baker's bicycle giving the Nazis a big clue where to start.

Jacques' heart hammered against his ribcage as he slipped through the narrow alleys of Ostend, the map folded tightly in his pocket. He knew that every step could be his last; the city was now a snare with Nazis lurking at every corner, their eyes sharp and searching. He could hear their heavy boots pounding the cobblestones, the snarling of their dogs, and the distant shouts that signalled their fury.

The bakery, once his sanctuary of warmth and doughy scents, had become a battleground. Soldiers overturned flour sacks and smashed his beloved ovens, ransacking the place for any trace of resistance. Jacques felt a pang of loss, not just for his livelihood but for the life he'd known, now crumbled like the crust of an over-baked loaf. He dearly hoped that the secret tunnel would remain untouched.

As dusk settled over the town, the search intensified. The German officers dispatched patrols down every street, and their ruthless efficiency left no stone unturned. Jacques' name echoed through the air, whispered by the sea breeze – Jacques Dumont, the baker, the traitor.

He watched from a resistance hideout, a cramped attic above the abandoned fishmonger's shop. Thoughts were now filled with a cold calculation born of necessity. He knew the risks; his identity was "burned", his face etched into the minds of his pursuers.

In the cloak of evening, Jacques made his move. He knew Wout would be at his usual haunt – a dimly lit tavern where the resistance often whispered their secrets. Jacques approached, cap pulled down low; his charismatic smile now a weapon of deception, masking the turmoil churning within him.

"Evening, Wout," Jacques said, materialising beside the man who held his daughter's fate in his hands. His voice was even, betraying none of the urgency that gripped him.

Wout looked up, startled, his grey eyes narrowing. "You shouldn't be here," he hissed, glancing around warily.

"Neither should you," Jacques retorted, "if you value your neck. But we have unfinished business."

Wout's gaze flicked towards the door, assessing the risk. "So what happened to just taking the photographs? I said *no heroics*, and I'm guessing you've taken something that's really pissed off Fritz! You got something big?" he surmised.

"I did," Jacques confirmed. "Now it's your turn. I need those orphanage files, Wout. My daughter, Kamia."

"Shh!" Wout cut him off sharply, his eyes darting to the entrance. "Not here. It's too dangerous."

"Then give me your word," Jacques pressed, the desperation he felt sharpening his tone. "Promise me you'll get me what I need."

Wout leaned back, studying Jacques with calculated interest. "I'll see what I can do. But right now, you need to disappear."

"Trust me, I intend to." Jacques' reply was a whisper, his resolve hardening like steel. This was the man who stood between him and the truth about Kamia. He couldn't afford to let Wout slip through his fingers — not when he was so close.

"Be careful, Dumont," Wout warned, a rare flicker of concern crossing his features. "They won't stop until they find you."

"Nor will I," Jacques vowed, his mind set.

"Meet me in the snicket in three minutes," said Wout, a glimmer of optimism in his eyes.

Jacques could only hear the pulse of his own heartbeat as he stood in the damp, shadowed alleyway, the night air thick with the menace of betrayal. Wout's silhouette loomed before him, a ghostly figure backlit by the flickering street lamp.

"Give it to me," Wout demanded, his voice low and threatening. "The cargo, Jacques. Hand it over or I swear, I'll turn you in." His grip tightened around Jacques' elbow.

The glint of optimism turned to malice in Wout's eyes. Jacques felt the weight of the stolen map pressed against his chest, where he'd tucked it inside his jacket — a fragile barrier between life and a bullet. His fingers twitched, itching to curl into fists.

"Turn me in?" Jacques' voice was a hoarse whisper, laced with incredulity and anger. "After everything—"

"Business is business," Wout retorted coldly. "You're compromised. The Gestapo will tear this town apart until they find you. And if handing you over saves my own skin ..." He trailed off, leaving the threat hanging like a noose.

Jacques clenched his jaw, the bitter taste of disillusionment flooding his mouth. He knew then that the map inked with secrets was his only lifeline; his bargaining chip in a game where the rules were written by traitors and tyrants.

"Keep your threats, De Vries," Jacques spat out, backing away into the darkness. "I'll take my chances." His mind raced with the realisation that his time in Ostend had run out. There was no path left but escape.

As footsteps echoed in the distance, a sign of the Nazi patrols already scouring the streets, Jacques turned on his heel and vanished into the labyrinth of Ostend's back alleys. With each step, he forced himself to accept the harrowing truth: Kamia, his beacon of hope in a world gone mad, was now cast adrift in the storm of war. He would have to leave her fate to the hands of destiny – at least for now.

The moon hung low in the sky, offering little in the way of reassurance or consolation. And yet he was out of options. Kamia needed her father alive – and staying in Ostend was tantamount to certain death. His thoughts whirled with plans to cross the Channel, to find sanctuary amidst the Allied forces, to fight. Only there, away from the reach of the Third Reich, could he hope to leverage the map's intelligence for something greater than his own survival.

"Survive," he whispered to the night, a prayer for himself, for Kamia, for all souls ensnared in the conflict. "Just survive."

With one last look at the town that had become his battlefield, Jacques steeled himself for the journey ahead. He would make his way to safer lands, clinging to the hope that when the war's cruel tide receded, it would reveal a path back to his daughter.

And with that, Jacques Dumont, the charismatic baker, a father turned resistance fighter, slipped away into the embrace of the dark, driven by the fervent wish that somewhere, somehow, little Kamia Dumont would endure this storm.

The worn leather of his satchel pressed cold and reassuring against his side. Having "borrowed" another bike, Jacques pedalled as cautiously and as quietly as the frame would allow. The narrow alleys were a maze of darkness and danger, but Jacques navigated them with the precision of a man who had no choice but to master his fear.

The cool night air carried the distant sounds of German patrols – boots and vehicles on rough streets, the clatter of weapons, voices stern with authority. Jacques' pulse quickened. He ducked into a recessed gateway as the beams of a searchlight swept past, briefly illuminating the bricks that had once felt like home. He waited, breath taut in his chest, until the light moved on and the shadows reclaimed him.

He emerged with calculated caution, pushing the bike forward, the rubber of the tyres soundless against the pavement. Every sense was heightened, every rustle of wind a potential alarm. The map, folded and hidden within the innermost pocket of his sturdy leather coat, was both his lifeline and a beacon for peril. The weight of it was a constant reminder of what was at stake – of Wout's betrayal, of his daughter's uncertain fate, of the resistance's desperate need for victory.

Another patrol rounded the corner ahead, their silhouettes stark against the faint glow of a streetlamp. Jacques retreated silently, pulse racing, his mind whirring with contingency plans. He knew these streets like the back of his hand, a skill born from years of delivering bread and smiles, now repurposed for eluding death. He took a narrow passage, barely more than a gap between buildings, where laundry hung like ghosts and whispered secrets of the lives they shrouded.

The Germans were thorough, their hunt methodical, but Jacques meandered in their midst – a whisper of defiance with the face of an Aryan, moving unseen, unheard. The irony was not lost on him; his appearance had been a protective cloak, a deceptive veneer that allowed him to walk amongst wolves. Now, this fame would be his undoing.

As he reached the outskirts of Ostend and the houses thinned, he began pedalling more powerfully through open fields and the distant promise of escape. Jacques' hands still welded to the handlebars, his resolve hardened, barely feeling the lactic acid in his thighs. This was it – the precipice of survival or capture; life or death. With one last glance behind him, where his past lay scattered and broken, wondering if he would ever return home.

The metallic click of the pedals was a signal to the night: Jacques Dumont would not be taken quietly. He still pedalled with fervour, starting to feel the muscles in his legs burning with effort and adrenaline. The map to Allied hands, the war to be fought from safer ground, and staying alive for his daughter's sake – it was all that drove him now.

His figure, a fleeting shadow against the dark tapestry of the Belgian countryside, disappeared into the night, swallowed by the vastness of a world at war. In his wake, the city of Ostend remained, its streets haunted by the ghost of a baker who once crafted bread and hope in equal measure.

Chapter 5:
Finding the Comet – 1942
(Jacques, aged 27)

Jacques Dumont's legs pumped the pedals of the bicycle with a desperate rhythm, propelling him through the veins of the Belgian countryside. The night cloaked him in its protective shadows as he avoided the main roads like a hunted animal steering clear of traps. His breath came out in quick, frosty puffs, visible only when the occasional moonbeam broke through the dense canopy of clouds.

Eyes darting left and right, Jacques' every sense was honed to detect danger. Even the slightest aberration – a snapped twig or a brief rustle in the underbrush – set his heart hammering against his ribcage. He was a man scarred by oppression, his charismatic smile replaced by a hard-set line, his piercing blue eyes scanning for threats instead of making connections.

The soft glow of an approaching car's headlights instantly transformed him from a conspirator on the run into prey. With well-honed reflexes, he veered off the path, muscles tensing as he threw himself and his bike into the thick tangle of undergrowth at the roadside. Holding his breath, he lay still, the Aryan features that usually served him well in evading suspicion now hidden beneath the brush.

Jacques remained motionless long enough to hear the car's engine fade into silence before he dared emerge. His lean body was coiled tight, ready to spring back into concealment at the slightest hint of discovery. But there was nothing – only the oppressive silence of the night returned.

Just as his grip on the handlebars relaxed slightly, the stillness was shattered by the distant crackle of machine-gun fire. The sound clawed at his insides, each shot echoing the beat of his racing heart. His mind reeled with the possibilities. Had they found his unit? His gut twisted with the guilt that Marcel and the others might be executed because of his recklessness.

The relentless uncertainty gnawed at him, but Jacques couldn't afford the luxury of grief or speculation – not yet. He heaved his bike back onto the path, the map hidden among his belongings feeling heavier than lead. It was not just paper; it was hope – a potent antidote to more death and destruction.

With renewed urgency, Jacques mounted his bicycle once more. The cold metal beneath his hands grounded him; the familiar feel of the grips a reminder of his purpose. He pedalled forward, the ghostly echoes of gunfire spurring him on into the depths of the night, towards his destination: Brussels. Distance: 134 kilometres.

Jacques Dumont's breaths came out as mist in the cold air, his legs pushing the pedals in a steady rhythm, a silent mantra against the terror that gripped him. The moon, a thin crescent in the ink-black sky, offered scant light, its silver edge intermittently cutting through the clouds.

Every shadow was an enemy, every rustle a threat. When hunger clawed at his stomach, he became a thief in the night, hands quick and silent as he snatched apples from a slumbering orchard. He rapidly gnawed on the fruit, before dispatching the core and returning to the feat of endurance he had embarked upon.

Water was scarce, and so Jacques turned to nature's offerings. He dropped to his knees beside a cattle trough, the reflection of a desperate man staring back at him from the murky surface. He scooped the water with cupped hands, the liquid tainted with the taste of earth and iron – it was survival distilled to its most basic element.

Skirting the prying eyes of Bruges, by sense of direction, Jacques clung to country lanes – it would add extra distance but the fewer witnesses to a suspiciously lone cyclist in the dead of night, the better.

As daybreak neared and with Bruges well behind him, the landscape took on a grey hue, the first signs of dawn stretching its fingers across the horizon. Panic set in. Jacques veered off the road, wheels crunching over fallen leaves and twigs as he sought refuge in the woods. With swift motions born of necessity, he camouflaged the bike under branches and leaves, his actions almost reverent in their precision.

Exhaustion pulled at his limbs, beckoning him to rest, but fear was a merciless taskmaster. He settled into the hollow embrace of a disused barn on the far side of the wood, the scent of must and old hay mingling in the air. Eyes closed, Jacques willed sleep to come, but it was elusive at best. Every creak of the aged wood, every whisper of the wind through cracks in the walls, sent adrenaline coursing through his veins.

The hours crawled by; the sun a silent observer to his vigil. As light seeped through gaps in the barn's timbers, Jacques' mind played tricks on him. Were those human shadows? Was that the murmur of voices plotting his capture? He curled up in the darkest of corners and prayed.

Finally, as the orange hues of dusk painted the sky, Jacques emerged from his hiding place. His movements were deliberate, cautious – a gazelle anticipating the ambush of hunters. The bike, once his ally in flight, now felt like a cumbersome companion as he released it from its leafy hide.

With the cloak of night descending once more, Jacques mounted his bicycle. The chain groaned under the strain. He looked across fields into the distance, where the lights of Ghent loomed.

He would skirt them, a ghost passing unseen, for capture meant death – or worse, betrayal of the cause. The map hidden among his belongings was not just paper; it was the lifeblood of resistance, and he, Jacques Dumont, was its courier.

As the first stars blinked into existence overhead, Jacques pedalled onwards, the night swallowing him whole, his journey a tightrope between hope and despair.

Jacques' legs were less reliable now, each pedal stroke a crescendo of pain arcing through his weary muscles. He endured the sharp sting of blisters forming on both buttocks, from the small chafes of every pedal stroke multiplied a thousand times. That night, Jacques spent eleven hard hours in the saddle, stopping only briefly to steal fruit and lap the water from roadside puddles

Finally, the outskirts of Brussels loomed before him; an urban maze that promised peril at every turn. As dawn threatened to expose him, Jacques sought sanctuary among the tangled roots of a beautiful ancient oak tree as it stood watch over a thick hedgerow.

Time crawled by, its passage marked only by the shift of shadows across the forest floor. Jacques huddled there, wet leaves clinging to his skin, the stench of sweat and fear permeating the air around his filthy form. Nevertheless, he had learned to be comfortable with adversity, and small blessings crossed Jacques' mind. *At least I'm not sat on that bloody saddle any more*, he mused.

As dusk approached, Jacques unfolded from his cramped refuge, having made a decision. The bike, which had borne him through the night, now seemed like a glaring beacon of suspicion. With a final pat to its worn saddle, Jacques concealed it in the hedgerow and happily turned his back on it.

The city was a different beast at night – a slumbering giant that held secrets in every alleyway. Jacques skulked along the fringes, another shadow among many, his eyes scanning the darkened streets with an intensity that belied his exhaustion. At last, he arrived at a nondescript house that was indistinguishable from its neighbours, save for the secrets it kept.

For an hour he watched, crouched behind a rusted automobile, as the ordinary life of Brussels unfolded unaware of the drama at its core. No glint of binoculars from the windows, no telltale signs of surveillance; just the occasional passing-by of oblivious citizens. His heart thudded a warning, but desperation propelled him forward.

He knocked — a soft, uneven rhythm that spoke of coded urgency. The door cracked open, and in the gap that appeared, Jacques whispered the phrase that would either save him or seal his fate. "Has grandmother's appetite returned?"

"Ah," came a hushed female voice, rich with relief. "She eats a little more every day." The door swung wider and Jacques slipped inside, ushered into the sanctuary of resistance.

Once the front door was bolted behind them, Jacques found himself standing in a very ordinary hallway, facing a very ordinary staircase. The woman who had greeted him proceeded to dismantle the first three stairs to reveal a short passageway into the bowels of the house, which opened up into a hidden room. She gestured for Jacques to enter, and reassembled the staircase behind him.

The hidden room was a hive of subdued activity, with familiar faces emerging from the shadows. Jacques' presence sparked a ripple of muted celebration. Words were exchanged in fervent whispers, updates and stories traded like contraband goods, each morsel of news devoured with hungry anticipation.

"We received your letter, Jacques. Looks like you've been busy!

"Brussels stands strong," they assured him, their voices laced with pride.

"And news from Ostend?" Jacques queried, anxiety sharpening his tone.

"Groupe G remains intact," came the response, though the tension in their shoulders told a tale of narrow escapes and close calls. The atmosphere was suffused with camaraderie and shared purpose – a testament to the bonds forged in the furnace of occupation.

As they clustered around, Jacques felt the weight of his solitude lift, replaced by the friendship of those who understood the cost of freedom. They were all architects of shadows, sculpting a silent rebellion. And tonight, in this hidden corner of Brussels, they revelled in the triumph of one man's journey through the perilous night.

Jacques' fingers trembled as he unfolded the creased map, the lines and markings dancing before his eyes under the flickering candlelight. The scent of roasted rabbit mingled with the earthy notes of black-market wine, a stark contrast to the odour of fear that had clung to him for days.

"Here," he said, voice hoarse from fatigue, pointing at the intricate web of routes sprawled across the paper. "U-boat movements, precise locations, call signs, schedules." His eyes met those of his comrades, their faces etched with intensity in the dimly lit room.

Elise Vignol (codename "Lily") leaned forward, her gaze locked on Jacques' face rather than the map. She saw beyond the grime, weariness and poor personal hygiene, glimpsing the raw determination within him.

Lily's outer appearance was average and unexceptional in every way. Brown hair pinned back in the usual style, two simple stud earrings, the lack of make-up showing that she had no money or means, dressed in a well-worn brown jacket and skirt.

But Lily was smart. Maybe the smartest conspirator of them all. Because every part of her appearance was intentional. Lily could blend in everywhere.

And Lily's banal exterior belied fierce resistance fervour flowing through her veins. She could sniff out traitors by merely observing their posture. She could source paperwork, identity cards and favours from a trusted network. This woman was the doyenne of the whole Brussels underground.

Meeting Jacques that night, a charismatic storyteller, she thought, and much more presentable after a shave and shower, the light accentuated his jawline and Lily's heart twisted with a familiar ache – admiration blending into something deeper; something more perilous than any resistance operation.

"Remarkable," she murmured, her fingertips brushing against Jacques' as she studied the charted depths of the Atlantic. "This could change everything."

"Indeed," one of the resistance members whispered, his voice laced with urgency. "We must protect this intelligence – and you, Jacques. You're too valuable now."

Jacques nodded, the weight of responsibility settling on his shoulders. As the conversation turned to logistics and hideouts, Jacques caught Lily's eye once more. Their connection was electric, charged with the adrenaline of the moment and the unspoken promise of intimacy. Yet, even as her touch ignited a fire within him, Jacques' thoughts strayed to England, to the long journey that lay beyond these walls.

Later, when the room lay silent save for the soft breathing of two lovers, Jacques and Lily had found solace in each other's arms. It was a fleeting reprieve, forged in the crucible of war —an attraction that burned bright for now. They slept deeply, naked limbs entwined together, in a tight embrace.

Morning came all too soon, and with it, the renewed gravity of their situation. The map, now spread across a rickety table, beckoned them with its coded secrets. Jacques' hand hovered over the North Atlantic, where the promise of thwarting enemy submarines held the power to tip the scales of war.

"Getting this to the British ..." Jacques began, his resolve steeling.

"Is our top priority," Lily finished, her voice resolute. "But we must be swift, Jacques. Every moment counts."

Jacques locked eyes with her as he finished his second café au lait of the day, sensing the weight of her loyalty, the depth of her commitment to the cause. Together, they were cogs in a vast machine of resistance, each turn bringing them closer to victory — or betrayal.

"Then we waste no time," Jacques declared, folding the map with practised care, concealing it within the safety of his faithful jacket. "Every second we hold this is a second too long."

The room pulsed with silent agreement; the air thick with the anticipation of action. This was no longer just about survival — it was about striking back, about delivering hope through the perilous channels of war. And for Jacques Dumont, it was about navigating the treacherous waters of allegiance and desire.

"Time is against us," he said, his voice low but firm as he turned to face Lily. "I must get to England, join the Royal Navy. Fight them on their own turf." He allowed himself a moment's vulnerability, his gaze searching hers. "The Nazis have taken everything from me. If they find me here ... I'm as good as dead."

Lily watched him with an intensity that belied her nondescript appearance. She nodded, her chestnut hair catching the sunlight streaming through the window. "You will not make that journey alone," she replied, her tone imbued with a quiet strength that commanded attention. "I've orchestrated safer passages for others; I can do it for you."

"Through Spain?" Jacques asked, a note of incredulity in his voice. The route was fraught with danger, crawling with informants and checkpoints.

"Exactly," Lily affirmed, her keen eyes never leaving his. "La Ligne Reseau is our contribution, Jacques. We've guided many to safety. You'll be one more, Jacques. But we must be careful, smart and lucky."

"Across the Pyrenees, then," Jacques mused aloud, the words tasting of adventure and peril all at once. His mind raced, picturing the rugged mountains that stood as silent sentinels between subjugation and freedom.

"Once in Bayonne, we'll reach out to the British consulate in Spain. They'll listen to you, they'll see the value of what you carry." Lily's words were like a lifeline thrown across the abyss of uncertainty that yawned before him.

"Thank you ... let's do this." He was brimming with confidence in Lily, and to have company on the voyage would increase his chances a thousandfold. Jacques' heart pounded with the promise of action.

That afternoon they ventured out into the muted buzz of a city under occupation, slipping unnoticed through the busy

Brussels streets. The city library loomed ahead, its neoclassical façade a mask for the knowledge that lay dormant within its walls.

"Remember, you're Jean-Pierre Bertillon now," Lily reminded him, her tone clipped with the urgency of their masquerade.

"An academic," Jacques mused, rolling the alias around his tongue. He had played many roles in this war, but none so cerebral.

The librarian looked down her nose at them, her disdain for Jacques' supposed field of study evident in the curl of her lip. "What use are African studies at a time like this?" she scoffed moodily. But Jacques met her gaze squarely, eyes unflinching, drawing on his command of language to parry her thinly veiled insults.

"Colonial socio-geographic development is vital to understanding the current global conflict," he countered smoothly in Flemish, almost believing the lie himself. Lily's approving nod was subtle, but to Jacques, it was a roar of applause.

Books in hand, they retreated to the safety of a shopping spree to gather the rest of his disguise. A tweed jacket here, a pair of spectacles there – each piece a fragment of Jean-Pierre Bertillon's persona. As they worked, their movements became a dance, a silent language that only they understood.

"How do I look?" Jacques asked, gripping his lapels and prancing around with an air of scholarly austerity.

"Like the most handsome lecturer I've ever seen," Lily giggled, her eyes lingering.

Back home, in the cramped space of their temporary refuge, they were more than lovers; they were friends. And as Jacques looked into Lily's eyes, he saw not just the pain they both carried, but the possibility of solace, even if only for a fleeting moment.

With the glare of five bright candles illuminating their workspace, Jacques and Lily sat hunched over his trusty black leather coat as it lay spread across the table before them. It had borne the brunt of Jacques' escape, protecting him from the brambles in roadside ditches and providing warmth whilst he slept in the Flanders' countryside, but the jacket had proven to be surprisingly durable and after a good wipe with a flannel of warm water seemed as strong as ever. Lily couldn't help but smile when Jacques had pranced about the room like a peacock, bragging how sharp and unique he looked, sporting a classic coat with that "lived-in" look. Now, with the jacket turned inside out and Lily by his side, Jacques warily grasped the razor blade. It flashed and glinted, slicing through the stitches with precision – a silent partner in their conspiracy. Each thread gave way reluctantly, fraying under the tension of their task. "Careful," whispered Lily, her breath warm against his ear as she steadied his hand. "We can't afford even the smallest tear." Jacques nodded, the weight of the map pressing against his thoughts like the cold steel of a gun barrel. With the lining peeled back, and Lily now relocating to sit provocatively on his lap, they slipped the precious paper inside. Lily's fingers moved deftly, laying strips of fabric over the map to muffle any betraying sound. Her eyes, sharp and focused, never left the task. Jacques, in contrast, was completely sidetracked and couldn't help but wrap his arms around her waist, kissing her neck tenderly whilst she worked to stitch the lining back in place.

"Done," she announced, with a final cut of the thread, her voice barely above a murmur. The jacket now appeared innocuous, its lethal contents invisible to all but those who knew where to look.

"Let's move onto your papers," said Lily, trying to resist the pleasure of having her neck kissed by the handsome academic.

Soon their forgery work was complete. "We should get some rest for tomorrow," Lily suggested softly, as their lips met once more.

Jacques led Lily to the sparse comfort of his room.

"Tomorrow, we head for the mountains," he said, the words heavy with the gravity of their journey.

"Tonight, we have each other," Lily whispered back.

And in that small room, with forged papers and a map hidden away, Jacques and Lily found another night's respite from the war outside.

The night was a shroud, and Jacques Dumont wore it like a second skin. Beneath the cloak of darkness and breathing slowly, he slipped from the bed sheets that cocooned Lily, silently clothed himself and descended the drainpipe with the agility of a cat burglar. Tonight was not about espionage or sabotage; it was personal — a father's quest to unearth the whereabouts of his daughter, Kamia.

Brussels slumbered under an oppressive occupation, and danger prowled the streets in the form of German Feldgendarm, their jackboots echoing through empty piazzas and along bare pavements. Jacques' heart pounded against his ribs, not from exertion but the raw fear of capture. He navigated the maze of shadows, each step deliberate, avoiding the pools of light spilling from the sporadic streetlamps.

The town hall loomed before him, a fortress of bureaucracy by day, now a silent monolith guarding its secrets. Jacques circled to the rear entrance, where only a single lock stood between him and the answers he sought. The lock gave way with the soft snap of his crowbar.

Thanks to efficient signage, the colonial records were clearly situated on the first floor. The air was stale, heavy with the weight of countless dusty files documenting lives and lies. Jacques flicked on his torch, a narrow beam of light slicing through the room. Drawers slid open with the squeak of old metal, and he rifled through them, searching for any trace of Kamia Dumont.

"*Qui est là?*" A voice startled Jacques, and his torchlight quivered. An ageing security guard emerged, his uniform hanging loosely on his stooped frame, the lines on his face etched with years of service and suspicion. He clutched a baton, more for support than as a weapon.

"Silence … please," Jacques implored, his whisper urgent. "I mean no harm."

"*Espion?*" The guard's grip on the baton tightened, wavering between duty and uncertainty.

"*Non, un père,*" Jacques said, his blue eyes locking with the guard's. "My daughter, she has been taken from me. I am trying to find her." His voice broke with the sound of desperation and hope, laying bare the raw ache in his chest.

The guard studied Jacques, the father's plea resonating with something paternal within him. Would he sound the alarm?

"*Ma fille est disparu aussi,*" the guard murmured, a distant look crossing his features. "I have not seen her since the Nazis arrived." His whisper was tinged with heartbreak. After what felt like an eternity, he lowered his baton. "If I find anything ... I will send word to the underground here in Brussels ... but you must go ... they say that thousands of unknown *métis* children were taken from the Congo into Belgian care, all without proper names and records ... you're searching for a needle in a mixed-race haystack, my friend."

"Yes, I know ... and from one father to another, you know I won't stop until I find her," Jacques replied with a long exhale, and with it the admission of just how futile tonight's search would be.

With a shake of his head, Jacques thanked the guard and slipped away, retracing his steps with the same stealth that had taken him there, every shadow now an accomplice in his escape. Clambering back up the drainpipe, Jacques' mind churned with the night's events – another dead end; another day without Kamia.

Re-entering the safety of his room, the map hidden in his coat seemed to mock him with its promise of purpose. But tonight, it was not U-boats or supply lines that haunted Jacques Dumont; it was the absence of his daughter – the hole in his world that no act of valour could fill.

The early morning light had barely begun its crawl across the rooftops of Brussels when a sudden rap at the door shattered the stillness of the safe house. Thankfully, Jacques was already dressed and packed for the journey, as a drab university lecturer. The sound spiked his adrenaline. A glance exchanged with Lily told him she too recognised the danger. The calculated rhythm of the knock was unmistakably that of authority – the Feldgendarm.

Panic surged through the resistance comrades, but it was the well-rehearsed drill practice that took over. Voices hushed to whispers as they scattered, each assuming their role in the cover story crafted for such moments. Books were opened, kettles set to boil; the illusion of an ordinary household rapidly assembled.

Lily's hand found Jacques', her grip firm, pulling him towards a hidden narrow staircase that led to the attic. "Upstairs, now," she hissed, the urgency in her voice matched by the determination in her eyes. Her face, usually a mask of composure, betrayed a flicker of fear as they ascended into the shadows above.

In the cramped space of the attic, dust motes danced in shafts of light piercing through the slats. There was no time for hesitation. Lily pushed aside a false panel beside the chimney breast revealing a gap just wide enough for a body to squeeze through. Below, the persistent knock grew more insistent, the demand for entry echoing ominously in the roof space.

"Go!" Jacques urged, his heart thudding against his ribcage. With the agility born of necessity, he followed Lily into the void, feeling the rough edges of brick and wood scrape against his skin. They emerged onto the neighbouring flat rooftop, the expanse of Brussels sprawling before them like a labyrinth of survival.

They descended a fire escape ladder into the adjacent garden, the earth soft and yielding beneath their feet. The air was crisp, the scent of damp soil mingling with the vestiges of their adrenaline. The sound of soldiers on the neighbouring street reached their ears, the search party drawing nearer, their German commands cutting through the morning air.

With every step towards the back alley, Jacques' muscles tensed, ready to spring into action should they be spotted. But fortune, it seemed, was on their side this day. The alley was deserted, save for the stray cats that darted away at their approach.

Jacques glanced at Lily; her chestnut hair attractively untidy from their escape. There was no time for words of gratitude or relief. They moved with purpose, their strides matching in rhythm as they navigated the intricate web of side streets that would lead them to the train station.

Their route passed by another safe house for Lily to collect two more fugitives - British airmen who she would also be chaperoning through France.

As they slipped into the crowd milling about the ticket hall, Jacques allowed himself a shallow breath. Amongst the sea of faces, they were invisible, just four more souls amidst the bustle of war. The whistle of an arriving train sounded like a promise, its steam billowing to the roof above their heads. Jacques' thoughts turned to the map concealed within his coat - a secret cargo that carried the weight of hope for thousands.

Chapter 6:

1932 (Jacques, aged 17)

Slinking through the dense underbrush, every snapped twig a shout of warning, every rustle of leaves a siren. The moon hung low, a pale witness to his clandestine movements as he navigated the familiar yet treacherous path to their secret meeting place.

He paused, listening intently. Nothing but the night chorus of the Congo – cicada, the distant call of a nightjar, the soft hoot of an African wood owl. Reassured, he moved on, his blond hair a stark contrast against the dark foliage, making him all too aware of his visibility in the moonlit night.

Finally, the clearing came into view, the silhouette of their baobab tree standing sentinel at its edge. And there, enfolded by shadows, was Ana. Her presence was like a balm to his anxious spirit, melting away the words of caution and replacing all Jacques' fears with fondness and love. She stood poised, her braids catching the moonlight, reflecting back a world of secrets and silent promises.

"Ana," he whispered, barely audible over the thumping in his chest.

She turned towards him, her features softening. "Jacques," she replied, her voice a hushed caress that wrapped around him with the warmth of the equatorial air.

They met in two strides, their bodies colliding with the desperate urgency of those who know their time is stolen. Their kiss was a dangerous dance; a mingling of fear and longing that tasted bittersweet.

"Your father ...?" Ana began, pulling back just enough to search Jacques' face for signs of danger.

"Sleeping," Jacques assured her, his blue eyes scanning the darkness beyond her for any sign of watchful eyes. "And Namiri?"

"Believes I'm staying with the healer's daughter." Ana's lips quirked up in a hint of mischief, a brief flicker of rebellion against the oppressive shroud of their reality.

"Every moment is a risk, Ana. If we're discovered ..." Jacques started, the weight of their potential doom pressing down upon him.

"Then let us make it worth the danger," she interrupted, her resolve steeling her voice. "You complete me, Jacques Dumont."

"Ana ... I've missed you ... I love you so much."

"I know, I know ... I feel it too."

Jacques marvelled at her courage, at how she stood defiant in the face of a world that would see them torn apart. It was this fire within her that drew him, that made the peril they faced seem a price worth paying.

"Let us escape, if only for tonight," he said, taking her hand and leading her towards the protective embrace of their jungle hideaway.

Love bloomed in the stolen hours of darkness, a testament to their unwavering connection amidst a society that demanded their separation. They shared whispered dreams and tender touches, carving out a sacred space where only they existed. In those fleeting encounters, they were not the son of a Belgian engineer and the daughter of a Congolese foreman – they were simply Jacques and Ana; two souls destined to be together for one whole lifetime.

Each parting brought the piercing reminder of the dawn that would inevitably rise, bringing with it the harsh light of reality. For now, though, they clung to the shadows, to each other, their love a silent act of defiance in a world that refused to understand.

Weeks of loving each other deepened into months. And then one day Ana found herself crouching behind a mud brick home on the edge of her village, heart pounding like a ngoma drum, one hand holding her stomach and the other, the wall. The rhythms of the village life throbbed around her, yet inside she was awash with silence – a deafening absence where the monthly assurance of her bleeding should have been. Her breath hitched as a nauseous sensation rose in her throat.

She glanced towards a fire where grandmother sat, her perceptive eyes scanning the young women as they ground maize. Ana could feel her gaze linger, could sense the knowing in those weathered lines that carved her face. The elder woman had seen this before; the signs of new life conceived in hushed whispers and hidden glances.

"Ana," she called, her voice steady but laden with unspoken questions.

Calmly straightening up and nonchalantly wiping traces of vomit from her lips, Ana did her best to hide the turmoil churning inside. Walking over, she offered a respectful nod, hoping a smile reached her eyes.

"You are well, child?" the wise mama enquired, peering at her closely.

"Y-yes, grandmother," she stammered, a bead of sweat trailing down her temple.

But her words faltered under the scrutiny, the truth burning at the edges of her tongue.

As night fell, Ana sought Jacques in their secret meeting spot. Their sanctuary within the jungle's embrace closed in as she uttered the words that would change everything.

"Jacques ... I'm with child."

Jacques' blue eyes, usually so full of fire, widened with bewilderment. They stood motionless, two teenage statues carved by fate's cruel hand, until Jacques found his voice.

"We'll find a way," he whispered fiercely, holding her trembling hands in his. "Together."

With the stealth of leopards, they approached the Dumont family home under the cloak of night. Jacques led Ana through the back door, into the warm kitchen where Sylvie Dumont was humming a tune whilst washing up. She beckoned the teenagers to sit with her at the kitchen table. Swan-like, Sylvie remained verbally calm but was emotionally paddling like crazy. The young lovers confessed everything.

The next evening, Jacques went to the village to locate Namiri, and found him relaxing after a hard day on the railroad. He pleaded with Namiri to follow him home. Namiri knew that something serious was occurring. Entering the Dumont family home, Jacques addressed everyone.

"Mother," Jacques began, his voice a tremulous thread. "Me and Ana – we need your help."

Sylvie's heart ached for the pair – although barely adults they were clearly made for each other. She turned to Namiri, who'd been listening intently. After a tense moment that felt endless, they both nodded, a silent pact forming between them.

"Ana will stay here," Sylvie declared with quiet resolve. "She is ours to protect now."

Namiri, her father, nodded sorrowfully in agreement. He had heard about the savage repercussions meted out on mixed-race families from Belgian and Congolese communities alike – it was unthinkable what would happen, and he feared for his daughter's safety.

***

Six months later, Ana gave birth, her muffled cries of maternal pain mingling with the monsoon rains outside. The room, filled with the soft murmur of prayers and encouragement, shone with the sweat of effort and the glow of imminent joy. Soon the cry of a newborn baby pierced the air, and it was met with a collective sigh – a sound heavy with relief and wonder.

Kamia Dumont entered the world cradled by love, her tiny fingers reaching for the warmth of her parents. Swaddled in blankets, the baby rested in their loving arms; although they were barely more than children themselves, yet they gazed upon their daughter with a love profound and fierce.

"*Elle est magnifique*," Sylvie whispered, tears spilling onto her cheeks. Henri stood beside her, pride swelling in his chest for the courage of his son and the strength of the girl who had become like a daughter to him.

Jacques held his girls close. He gently kissed Kamia's forehead, vowing silently to defy the heavens, if he must, to keep her safe. In that moment, the stakes of their forbidden love had never been clearer, nor the peril more acute.

That first year passed in the blink of an eye, and family life was blissful. Henri and Namiri continued to work the railroad. Sylvie looked after her family, and Jacques, Ana and Kamia became closer than any family had before. They shared every moment together; first smiles, sleepless nights, ailments and teething … and it only served to deepen their love. Jacques and Ana had passed through the education system, providing time for Ana to spend short periods away from Kamia to visit her family home, and Jacques ran errands in Léopoldville, pretending that he wasn't deeply in love with a local woman, and the father of a *métis* child. Kamia was growing into a healthy, happy toddler, with a full belly every night and all of the tickles, cuddles and amusement she wanted, from a close family who loved her very much.

Although Kamia spent these early months away from society, never playing with another child, at least she was safe from the outrage that her beautiful light brown skin would stir in the white members of society.

As the years passed by, Ana found friendship with a small group of Congolese mothers who all carried the heaviest of burdens: their children were neither black nor white. Shunned by both the indigenous and the European: a society that accused them of being little more than whores, seducing white men to commit a sinful act. These mothers worked valiantly to protect their beloved Eurafrican children from feeling the slur of being society's least. And they had each other.

For six years the family grew happily complacent in their contentedness and secrecy. With the love and attention of so many adults, Kamia was blossoming into a bright, capable and confident girl for her age.

Until that fateful day arrived – the day that all the mothers of *métis* children feared most.

The joy within the Dumont household was infiltrated by something more sinister. Whispers of a decree from the Belgian authorities slithered into their sanctuary, venomous and cold. The colonial puritanical patriarchy, driven by a mandate to sever the bonds of biracial families, to cleanse the colony of what they deemed impure.

"Interbreeding", they called it, a term spat out with derision and wrapped in the guise of national honour.

Jacques peered through the slats of the wooden shutters, his breaths shallow and rapid. The whisper of swaying laundry outside was a stark contrast to the heavy silence that hung in the air. He guessed who the traitors were – the white neighbours, their eyes narrow with suspicion as they cast glances towards the Dumont family home.

"Ana," he hissed, urgency lacing his voice. She materialised beside him, her presence both reassuring and heart-wrenching. "They've come for her."

Ana's eyes widened. She clutched her chest, struggling to breathe.

"*Non*, Jacques," her voice barely audible. "We cannot let them take her."

But even as she spoke, the dull rumble of a motor car approached; a trail of dust behind it served as a rhythmic omen of the devastation about to unfold.

And then it happened – a sharp rap on the door that shattered their world into fragments.

"*Ouvrez!* Open up in the name of the King!" came the authoritative bark. Jacques felt Ana's grip tighten around his arm; an anchor amidst the chaos.

The door swung open, and a trio of missionaries led by Father Dax himself barged inside, flanked by two gendarmes. Their eyes, cold and unyielding, immediately locked onto Ana, who cradled Kamia protectively against her chest.

"Hand over the child," Dax commanded, his voice devoid of compassion.

"Please," Jacques pleaded, stepping forward, his entire body coiled like a spring. "She is our daughter – you can't do this … she has rights … No!"

"Enough!" The missionary sliced through Jacques' words. "The law is clear. This infant is the work of the devil. A sin in the eyes of God, a disgrace to the great Belgian nation, and is to be repatriated to a safe institution. Our sisters will educate this *mulâtre* girl in Belgian culture and Christianity, away from the shame of the world. We have prepared these documents stating her parentage. Sign these papers of authorisation now. Fail to comply, and you'll never see her again."

With a suddenness that left them reeling, the men wrenched the six-year-old from her mother's arms, trying to drag her to the car. Kicking and punching, Kamia broke free and raced back to her father, wrapping her arms tightly around his waist, as he struggled in the grip of two powerful gendarmes.

"Quick, take my necklace, Kamia," snapped Jacques.

But Kamia was too distraught to comply. Her cries pierced the heavy air as two of the missionaries prised her thin brown arms from Jacques' waist, wrenching her from the home she loved, down the path and onto the back seat of the waiting car. With little choice but to comply for now, Jacques scratched a signature on the papers, along with his aunt's address in Ostend and his father's company initials, SNCC. They would need as many ties and clues to find each other as possible.

"Kamia! Kamia! Kamia!" Ana's scream was a raw echo of every parent's nightmare. Tears streaked down her face as she fought against the hands that restrained her.

"Let go of me!" Jacques' defiance was met with a shove that sent him crashing to the floor. His vision blurred as he looked up to see the white robes of the missionaries ghosting through his front door, slamming it behind them.

Within seconds, Ana raced over to lift Jacques from the floor. The pair of them bolted through the front door, determined to stop the car from leaving, but it was too late. The dusty cloud swept Kamia away into the distance.

"*Mon amour,*" Ana wept, her voice broken by devastation. They collapsed together on the front step of the porch, their embrace a fortress against the pain that threatened to consume them. Their beautiful daughter, the most precious part of their love, was gone.

In the aftermath, a suffocating silence filled the spaces where Kamia's laughter once was. Where they danced … where they read stories … where they nursed … where they talked … just silence.

Jacques and Ana sat motionless, their hearts hollowed out by grief. Their bond, once unbreakable, now insecure under the weight of their shared sorrow. Kamia's absence was a chasm between them, dark and deep.

"Where do we go from here?" Ana's voice was faint; a whisper lost in the void.

Jacques' blue eyes, usually so bright, were dimmed by tears unshed. He reached for Ana's hand, holding it as though it were the last lifeline in a sea of despair.

"Anywhere," he murmured. "Anywhere but here."

***

The heat of the Congolese sun bore down on the railroad office; a stifling air hanging heavy between Henri Dumont and his employers. The sweat on Henri's brow wasn't just from the climate; his job – and perhaps his son's future – hung by a thread thinner than the telegraph wires strung along the tracks outside.

"Please, you must understand," Henri implored, his voice a hoarse whisper of desperation. "I have worked with unwavering loyalty for years. My family needs me."

The railroad executives exchanged glances, their expressions as unreadable as the savannah plains. Finally, one of them, a man with a manicured goatee and a posh accent that seemed to mock the gravity of the situation, spoke up.

"Dumont, your work has always been exemplary. We'll turn a blind eye to your son's misdemeanours this time. But be warned, no more ... interracial incidents. There are enough damned 'mulattos' around here already, and however attractive they may physically be, we should never forget that they carry the determinants of the pure character of the black race."

"*Merci, merci infiniment,*" Henri breathed out, relief washing over him like the first rains after a drought. But as he left the office, his thoughts turned to Namiri Mbala, who hadn't been so fortunate. Sacked without ceremony, the middle-aged Congolese man now faced backbreaking labour on the coffee plantation, the colonial authorities stripping him of dignity and livelihood in one swift blow.

Meanwhile, Jacques and Ana, driven by the sharp sting of injustice and the constant ache of having Kamia snatched from them, had vanished into the dense embrace of the jungle. The foliage closed behind them, erasing their path as if they were never there, leaving only whispers of rebellion in their wake. They sought solace in isolation.

Days turned to weeks, and their jungle hideout showed no mercy. Its beauty was a façade masking the dangers lurking within its green depths. Fever gripped them both, malaria parasites swarming their bloodstream. Delirium twisted reality into a haze, and strength ebbed from their bodies with each shivering breath.

It was the Bambuti pygmy tribe, wanderers of the Congo, who found them – two feverish souls lying helpless among the roots of an ancient tree. With hands practised in the art of healing, they applied poultices to cool, and mixed potions from handpicked roots and leaves to ease the pain, chanting incantations that seemed to pierce the veil between worlds.

Time became a blur, measured only by the rise and fall of the sick lovers' chests as they fought against the invisible predator within. When at last their eyes opened, free from the haze of sickness, they found themselves cradled in the safety of Namiri's humble abode.

"Namiri," Jacques rasped, his throat raw, "how did we …?"

"Shh, rest now," the elder soothed, his presence a balm to their weary spirits. His gentle authority offered no rebuke, only the unspoken understanding of their plight.

In the silence that followed, pierced by the distant calls of the jungle, Jacques held Ana close. Their breaths synchronised, a silent vow that no force, man nor nature, would tear them asunder again. But even as they clung to each other, the shadows of the jungle loomed; a stark reminder of their vulnerability in the face of a world that demanded their separation.

Jacques' consciousness clawed its way back from the murky depths of fevered dreams, the sweat-drenched sheets a testament to his body's war against malaria. His mother's silhouette now hovered at Jacques' bedside, her hands clasped tightly as if in prayer. He squinted, trying to make sense of the room that seemed both familiar and alien. Jacques roused briefly to the awareness that he was back in the comfort of the Dumont family home.

"Mother?" His voice was a cracked whisper, the words barely escaping his lips.

"Shh, my dear boy," she replied, her eyes brimming with relief yet shadowed with sorrow. "You've been very ill."

"Ana," he gasped, the urgency surging through him like an electric current. "Where is Ana?"

His mother's face paled, her expression falling at the edges. In that moment, Jacques understood; the silent scream of loss echoed through every fibre of his being.

"Show me," he demanded, staggering out of bed, his legs weak but driven to move.

They arrived at the outskirts of Ana's village just as the last notes of a mournful chant floated on the breeze. The air was heavy with the scent of incense and the sombre rhythm of drums. Through tear-blurred eyes, Jacques watched as the villagers encircled a freshly covered grave, the wailing of human grief reaching skyward as if to carry Ana's spirit away from this earthly realm.

Her tribal funeral ceremony was coming to a close, and with it, a chapter of Jacques' life irreparably shattered in that moment. He stood there, devastated, rooted to the spot. How could he have let this happen? First Kamia … and now Ana … it was too much.

He had failed as a father to save his daughter.

He had failed to keep his soulmate alive.

And it was shame, the most insidious emotion of them all, that hurled Jacques into an abyss.

In the weeks that followed, grief became his constant companion, a dark shroud that neither sunlight nor the passage of time could penetrate. His thoughts shifted from depression to rage against the colonial authorities and their oppressive segregation that had crushed so many lives, including Ana and Kamia's.

Two months passed by and the clouds had not lifted, although he had found ways to mask the heartbreak.

It was in the dimly lit confines of a local bar where Jacques could forget; the amber spirit providing a temporary reprieve from his torment. There, amidst the clinking of glasses and the low hum of despondent conversations, he found kinship in a fellow drunk. Martin Spiessens – a rugged, unkempt journalist whose disdain for the establishment mirrored his own.

"Another round," Martin slurred, signalling the bartender with a crooked finger. "To damned oppressors and dickheads."

"May they rot," Jacques growled, downing his drink in one bitter gulp. Their eyes met in shared pain and purpose.

"Listen, lad." Martin leaned in, his breath heavy with the stench of alcohol. "We can sit here mourning till kingdom come, or we can bloody well do something about it."

"Anything," Jacques agreed, a vow etched into his core.

"Good." Martin nodded with a sly grin spreading across his face. "Because I have a plan, and it involves exposing these bastards for what they truly are."

Together they plotted, their scheming fuelled by a potent blend of fury and desperation. They were mavericks cast adrift in a world that had shown no mercy, and now they would seek a little revenge. For Ana, for Kamia, for every soul trampled under the boot of colonial tyranny, they would strike back. A little piece of justice wrenched from the clutches of those who wielded power with selfish indifference.

After a few days' planning, enough time for their headaches to subside, all was set. Spiessens' muscular frame crouched in the grounds, hidden by the shadow of a flamboyant tree, his breath shallow and controlled as he gripped the camera – a Kodak No. 1 Autographic – tight in his hands. The missionary school loomed before him, its whitewashed walls a stark contrast to the vibrant Congolese landscape. Sunlight glinted off the lens as he peered through it, waiting for the damning moment to reveal itself.

Jacques, pressing his body against the rough bark of an adjacent acacia, nodded at his comrade, his eyes hawkish behind the thick lenses of his spectacles. "There," he whispered hoarsely, as a door to the school swung open. "It's Dax."

The missionary, clearly identifiable in white robes, emerged, followed by a small Congolese boy. The child's uniform hung loose on his thin frame, the fabric worn and faded. Dax pushed the lad up against the wall, the boy's head bowed. After quickly scanning for onlookers, the missionary's aggression began knifing across the still air – a litany of accusations, each word a venomous strike: "*Sale negre!*"

Jacques dug his nails into the tree bark, anchoring him against the burning desire to rain punches on the chubby pink face of

Dax. Spiessens steadied himself, focusing the lens just as the missionary raised his hand.

"This hurts me more than it hurts you, boy," Dax justified. "In your name, Lord, I return the sinner to the righteous path." And with that, the slap landed hard, a sound far too loud for the quiet morning, with enough force to launch the schoolboy sprawling across the dust. The shutter clicked incessantly, barely audible over the child's stifled cry. The physical assault continued with a kick to the boy's gut, leaving him motionless. Every blow captured on film.

"Got it," Spiessens murmured, a cold satisfaction settling in his chest as he captured several more images, each one a testament to the cruelty inflicted upon the innocent.

"Let's move," Jacques urged, his gaze sweeping the area for unwanted observers. Together, they slipped away, unseen shadows amidst the foliage. "Take these and go public, Martin – take them down for good."

"I will," he promised.

***

The Dumont home was a tumult of emotion as Sylvie folded the last of their belongings into a trunk, her movements mechanical. Jacques watched his mother, her face so used to smiling, now bereft of emotion.

Henri entered, a telegram clutched in his calloused hands. "We have to go. Now. Everyone is needed back home." His voice trembled, betraying the gravity of their situation.

Jacques knew the implications. Europe was on a knife-edge, and now the blade threatened to cut them from their African refuge. There was no turning back, and without any indication of Kamia's whereabouts, he concluded that the best place to start searching for her would be the centre of Belgian colonial power and administration: Brussels.

***

"Namiri," Jacques called out, striding over the dusty ground towards the Mbala family dwelling. The stoic elder gingerly eased his creaking joints off the floor, to welcome his friends, the Dumonts, as they approached with laden arms. Jacques was the first to greet Namiri, with Henri and Sylvie close behind, each bearing items that whispered of their shared family life together: silver photograph frames, a cherished family timepiece, linens that once comforted Namiri's grand-daughter as she slept.

"Keep these safe … sell them if you need to – either for your own family, or to find Kamia," Henri instructed. "Let's pray we meet again in happier times, old friend."

Namiri nodded, accepting the offerings with a dignity that defied his recent demotion to coffee plantation labourer. "Bon voyage … until we meet again, my friends," he replied, his voice laced with uncertainty.

As the Dumonts boarded the train bound for Matadi port, Jacques looked back one last time, his vision blurring with tears. The Congo, with its unforgiving beauty and heartache, receded into the distance, leaving an indelible mark upon his soul. This was his home, with Ana, with Kamia.

The hissing of the locomotive drowned out the farewells, but not the silent vow that thundered in Jacques – to fight, to reclaim what had been torn from their grasp. With every mile that separated him from the land that had cradled his daughter and his soulmate, an ember of revenge within him flared hotter, the vengeance of a father who would stop at nothing to find his daughter.

I'm coming Kamia — your papa is coming to get you.

Chapter 7:
Riding the Comet – 1942
(Jacques, aged 27)

Jacques' senses heightened as he strode alongside Lily onto the bustling platform in Brussels. The scent of coal and iron filled the air, mingling with the sharp tang of fear that clung to his skin. He was acutely aware of their quartet – two men in nondescript long coats, collars turned up against the chill, trilby hats casting shadows over their anxious faces. Jacques' charming smile was a mask, practised and perfect, disguising the torrent of emotions within.

Each passer-by became a potential threat; every glance held the possibility of recognition. The words they all dreaded seemed to echo in Jacques' mind, a ghostly whisper waiting to materialise: "*Halt, wir sind die Gestapo, folge mir, du abschaum des widerstands.*" It would take just one slip, one curious eye, one lingering look to unravel everything.

Earlier, as dawn's light had barely touched the cobblestone streets, Jacques and Lily had retrieved George and Arthur, the two British airmen, from their temporary haven. With the gravitas of a seasoned operative, Lily distributed forged papers and passports like a general deploying her troops into battle. Her voice calm and motherly, she drilled the airmen on their cover stories.

"Remember, you are Louis de Poel and Mathieu Moreaux, students at the École des Beaux-Arts," she instructed, her eyes flicking back and forth between the airmen. When they responded, their accents butchered the beautiful language, turning French into an almost comedic display of English-public-schoolboy mockery.

With a swift decision born of necessity, Lily adapted their story. "You are now deaf artists," she declared, the corner of her mouth twitching in suppressed amusement. "Do not speak. If we are questioned, I will answer for you."

Now, as they waited for their train, Jacques watched the airmen nod in silent agreement, their expressions earnest but tinged with the absurdity of their predicament. They understood the stakes, yet the human moment shared in the shadow of danger was a brief respite from the crushing weight of their mission for freedom.

The train's whistle cut through the tension, signalling their departure. With a final glance at each other, they boarded, their hearts racing in tandem with the chugging of the locomotive. There was no turning back now; Paris awaited, along with the promise of danger and the hope of salvation.

The train's rhythmic clatter became a metronome to Jacques' accelerating heartbeat. Each click and clack on the tracks seemed to resonate with his pulse, a syncopated reminder of the risks that lay ahead. Lily sat across from him, her keen eyes scanning their compartment – a motley assembly of strangers, each lost in their own world, unaware of the silent drama unfolding before them.

George and Arthur, disguised as deaf artists, feigned disinterest in the scenery flashing by, yet their stiff postures betrayed a vigilance equal to Jacques'. Occasionally, their eyes would meet, exchanging a wordless language of solidarity and nerves stretched taut like violin strings.

As the outline of Quiévrain station at the French border emerged on the horizon, the air in the compartment grew thick with apprehension. Jacques' breaths became shallow, an attempt to calm the storm of anticipation swirling within. He felt his jacket's lining, reassuring himself that the map – his dangerous secret – remained undetected against his ribcage.

The train hissed to a stop at the border, and time seemed to slow to a crawl. The doors opened with a jolt, and a pair of Feldgendarmes stepped aboard, followed by *douaniers* with their piercing gaze and methodical movements. Jacques could hear his own blood thrumming in his ears as they drew nearer, the agents of occupation checking papers, probing for any sign of deceit.

"Votre papiers, s'il vous plaît," one of the officers demanded, his voice devoid of warmth.

With practised nonchalance, Jacques presented his documents, steadying his hands against the tremors that threatened to betray him. His thoughts fixated on the map, praying it would remain as silent and hidden as the secrets it held. Lily's voice cut through the tension, crisp and authoritative, fielding questions with an ease that made Jacques marvel at her composure under pressure.

Next to her, George and Arthur embodied statues, their faces blank slates of feigned ignorance. They avoided eye contact with the SS soldiers peering in through the windows, German shepherds at their sides sniffing the air for traces of fear or subterfuge.

"*Alles in ordnung*," the Feldgendarm eventually declared, handing back the papers with a disinterested flick of his wrist. As the officials moved on, Jacques allowed himself the smallest exhale – a fleeting whisper of relief quickly swallowed by the ever-present dread of discovery.

Silently, the resistance group shared a look of muted triumph. Yet the shadow of the SS, ever watchful on the platform, served as a stark reminder: they were still deep within the serpent's lair, and the slightest misstep could prove fatal.

The train lurched forward, wheels clacking against the rails in a rhythm that echoed the pounding heartbeats of its clandestine passengers. With each mile devoured beneath them, Paris loomed closer, promising both sanctuary and peril. Jacques' gaze lingered on Lily, her beautiful eyes scanning the compartment with the vigilance of a hawk – those same eyes that had shared physical intimacy just a few nights before. Beside her, George and Arthur feigned indifference, their bodies rigid with the strain of their silent charade.

As the countryside blurred past, a shiver of anticipation coursed through the cabin. They were moving again, free from the scrutinising eyes of the border guards — for now. The deceptive calm afforded by their departure from Quiévrain allowed only a momentary respite. A collective breath was drawn and held, as if to forestall the reality of the dangers still ahead.

The journey to Paris was a quiet affair, tension woven into the very fabric of the air they shared with unsuspecting travellers. All the while, Jacques felt the map's presence against his chest — a secret burden that weighed heavy upon him.

The Gare du Nord materialised from the haze of dusk, its grandeur reduced to a mere backdrop for the more pressing drama at hand. Lily was the first to rise as the train hissed to a stop, her movements purposeful yet discreet. She gestured to her companions, her expression taut with urgency.

"*Allez,*" she murmured, barely audible above the din of disembarking passengers.

They wove through the crowd with a laissez-faire that belied their inner turmoil. Lily led the way, her eyes darting between the faces in the throng and the uniformed soldiers who stalked the platforms like wolves among sheep.

"Here," she whispered, indicating a nondescript door marked "Personnel Only".

Jacques glanced over his shoulder, noting the proximity of patrolling soldiers, their boots echoing ominously on the stone floor. He reached for the handle, relieved to find it unlocked as planned. They slipped inside, away from prying eyes, enveloped by the musty scent of mops and cleaning fluid.

Without pausing, Lily guided them through the narrow space crowded with buckets and brooms. In the far corner, a sliver of light beckoned – a forgotten access door left ajar. It was their gateway to the anonymous network of Parisian streets.

The quartet emerged into the dimming light of evening, the cool air a sharp contrast to the warm fug of the station. They blended into the Parisian tapestry like shadows at sunset, disappearing amidst the hustle of city life.

"Keep close," Lily instructed, her voice low but clear.

With the setting sun as their ally, they navigated the side streets with caution. Paris might have been the City of Light, but for those who dared defy the occupiers, it was a landscape fraught with darkness and danger.

Stepping off the busy Rue de Clichy in the 9th Arrondissement, they entered a small courtyard, wearily climbing stone steps up to the first floor. Someone must have been observing them because the door of apartment 5 creaked open as they approached, its hinges complaining in the silence of the Parisian dusk. Each of the travellers was tired, yet anxious to know whether their safe house could be a trusted place to sleep. The way Lily and Paul greeted each other was a relief to her companions. And Paul turned to welcome each of them in turn. The old man's eyes glittered with satisfaction as he ushered them inside, the lines on his face deepening with a smile reserved for comrades in arms – or in this case, family.

"*Mon brave*," Paul murmured to Lily, pride lacing his voice as he pulled her into another loving hug. Jacques observed the exchange, noting the familiarity but unaware of the bond that tied these two souls together. It was Lily's father who stood before them, the architect of so many escapes, now harbouring them within the walls laden with secrets and whispers of resistance.

"*Merci*, Paul," Lily answered with a nod, her tone as business-like as ever despite the affectionate gesture.

They gathered around a modest wooden table as Paul served a simple meal of pot-au-feu, the steam from the hearty stew fogging up the lone window that overlooked Rue de Clichy, below. The warmth of the food, and its chef, did much to ease the tension of the day's adventure.

"Here's to small victories," Jacques toasted quietly, raising his bowl in a cautious celebration. They ate with an awareness that each mouthful carried them further on their journey —towards hope, towards freedom.

In the following days, the confines of the flat became both sanctuary and classroom. George and Arthur, the British airmen, took it upon themselves to tutor Jacques in the nuances of English — a language that could prove vital in the times to come. Their laughter at Jacques' initial attempts was good-natured, belying the gravity of their situation.

"Say it with me, old chap: 'I would like to serve in the Royal Navy,'" George instructed, his 'Home-Counties' accent lilting with gusto.

"Ahwoold laik to sev in ze Roy-al Nev-ee," Jacques parroted, his own accent thick and unyielding.

"Blimey, we've got our work cut out," Arthur chuckled, shaking his head.

"Less like a Belgian, more like Churchill," Lily teased, her eyes dancing with mirth as she watched their efforts.

But as the days passed, Jacques' determination shaped his tongue to the foreign sounds, his desire to join the Royal Navy fuelling his resolve. He spoke of his plan enthusiastically, revealing a burning need to play his part in the grander scheme — to strike back against the tide of tyranny that had swept across his homeland and his heart.

"Listen to me carefully," Jacques said one evening, his newfound English words slow but precise. "I want to serve. To fight. For freedom. For justice."

Lily watched him, a mix of admiration and something deeper flickering in her gaze. His commitment to the cause, his ability to inspire trust — it was what made Jacques not just an asset to the resistance but also a beacon of hope in the darkest of times. *You are a leader too*, she thought.

"*Vous serez formidable*, Jacques," Paul said, his eyes alight with a mixture of paternal pride and the knowledge of the treacherous path ahead.

Jacques nodded, aware that every lesson learned, every plan whispered beneath the veil of night, brought them closer to the perilous crossing into Spain — and into the unknown.

After a bittersweet farewell to Paul, and having made their way south without too much difficulty, Lily's group found themselves on a bustling platform at Bayonne station, the chugging of engines and hissing of steam weaving an undercurrent of urgency as Lily's eyes locked with Jacques' for what could be the last time. She reached out, her hand trembling slightly, to adjust the collar of his coat, a gesture that spoke volumes more than any farewell could. Her lips parted, but the words caught in her throat, silenced by the wave of emotion welling up inside her.

"Take care of yourself, Jacques," she managed at last, struggling to suppress her feelings, her voice barely above a whisper.

Jacques nodded, the weight of responsibility pressing down on him like a physical force. His blue eyes, so often alight with defiance, now expressed a depth of emotion he couldn't conceal. He glanced at Madame Bouvait, who stood ready with the bicycles, then back to Lily.

"*Je ne t'oublerai jamais*," he replied, his words carrying a promise that stretched beyond the war, beyond the perils that awaited.

"I'll never forget you, either," she echoed.

With a final squeeze of her hand, he winked his left eye and turned to swing his leg over the saddle of his bicycle, accelerating a little to catch up with the two British airmen who were weaving and wobbling down the road, giggling away to each other as they narrowly avoided yet another collision. Lily's heart twinged with a pain she hadn't anticipated, the sight of Jacques' retreating form etching itself into her memory.

That evening, hidden from prying eyes in the back room of a dimly lit café, whispers of daring and hope danced between the shadows. The Bayonne resistance had gathered; a motley crew bound by a common thread of defiance. They exchanged stories, each tale a patchwork piece of a larger tapestry of rebellion.

Jacques listened, the names and faces around him a testament to the reach of their cause. One man, whose face resembled the Congolese friends from his youth, leaned closer, his voice a low rumble that carried the warmth of shared history.

"Did you go to school in Léopoldville?" he asked, recognition sparking between them.

"Indeed," Jacques confirmed, the corners of his mouth lifting in a sad smile. "I had a friend there, Boboto Nganga. We called him Bobi."

"Ah, Bobi!" the man exclaimed, his eyes brightening. "Yes, I thought I recognised you! You know, Bobi made it to University of Cape Town – the first from Léopoldville to do so. A true role model for our people."

A swell of pride rose in Jacques' chest, mingled with a sharp pang of homesickness. But the news that followed sobered him instantly.

"And that missionary teacher: Father Dax ... he hid in Léopoldville after the scandal broke. Martin Spiessens exposed his vile deeds in the national papers from Matadi to Brussels. But justice has a way of finding the wicked. They found him one morning, lifeless, hanging from the flagpole outside the Colonial Ministry building."

Seriousness descended on their conversation with the unspoken understanding of tribal retribution. Jacques felt a chill despite the close quarters. Father Dax's death was a grim reminder of the darkness they all faced, yet in that darkness there shone a glimmer of justice.

"May it be a lesson to all oppressors," Jacques murmured, his voice hard with resolve. "We fight not just a war of guns and bombs, but a war against oppression in all its forms."

Heads nodded around the room, the collective spirit of the resistance galvanised by the tales of courage and sacrifice, and the promise of a world freed from the grip of fascism. Tonight, they were not just French, British or Congolese – they were allies in the truest sense, united in a battle that knew no borders.

Next evening, the sun dipped low, casting long shadows across the rural roads that led to Anglet. The three escapees, guided by Madame Bouvait, pedalled a few kilometres with a rhythmic consistency that had become second nature. The familiar burn in his thighs reminded Jacques of the escape from Ostend, and it was a welcome distraction from the weight of his thoughts now – the secrets he carried, the lives at stake, and the sharp absence of Lily's reassuring presence.

Madame Bouvait rode ahead, her silhouette steady against the encroaching dusk. Their destination loomed: a safe house where black market bounty promised a reprieve from the meagre rations they'd subsisted on during their perilous journey.

"Nearly there," she called back, her voice soft but carrying.

A sense of camaraderie settled over the three men as they dismounted, legs trembling not just from exhaustion, but also from the relief of another day survived. Inside, the aroma of rich stew and freshly baked bread enveloped them like a warm embrace. They ate in subdued celebration, each mouthful laced with the knowledge that moments of such simple pleasure were fleeting in these dark times.

As night swathed the world outside in its embrace, Jacques lay on a makeshift bed, his body heavy with fatigue, yet sleep eluded him. His mind replayed the words exchanged in hushed tones earlier that evening, the resistance fighters' stories intertwining with his own silent narrative. He understood that every step forward was etched in risk and resilience.

The following afternoon brought an air charged with anticipation. Their mountain guide, Florentino, arrived, his rugged features set in stern determination. Without preamble, he thrust a pair of espadrilles into Jacques' hands.

"Silence is our ally," Florentino gruffed. "These will muffle your steps."

Jacques examined the soft canvas shoes with soles made of twine, understanding their purpose beyond mere footwear – they symbolised the stealth required for the next leg of their odyssey. Slipping them on, he felt the ground through the thin soles, an intimate connection to the earth that would bear witness to their covert passage.

"Listen carefully to my instructions," Florentino continued, eyes scanning the men before him. "The Pyrenees are unforgiving. One misstep could cost us all dearly."

Jacques nodded, the gravity of the situation pressing down upon him like the mountains themselves. He looked to his companions, their expressions mirroring his resolve. They were ready.

Dusk settled over the quaint home of Madame Bouvait. Jacques, George and Arthur sat in tense silence, their gazes flitting towards Florentino with every creak of the floorboards, every rustle of the wind against the windowpanes. The berets perched atop their heads and the traditional Basque attire they wore felt like costumes for a play they were reluctantly cast in – one that could see them whisked off to a concentration camp if poorly performed.

Jacques' fingers traced the fabric of his jacket, a constant reminder of the weight he carried. It was more than just stitched leather and buttons; it held the future — a map sewn into the lining that could tip the scales of war. He kept it on despite the odd looks from Madame Bouvait, who was oblivious to the secret sewn within its threads.

A nod from Florentino pierced the stillness. It was time. They rose with rehearsed casualness, but adrenaline surged through Jacques' veins, pulsing with the urgency of their mission and the peril that lay ahead.

The cool air outside nipped at their exposed skin as they ventured into the shadows of the Pyrenees. The espadrilles muted their footsteps, each man a ghost, drifting through the underbrush. Jacques led the way, following closely behind Florentino's assured steps, feeling the land's contours through the thin soles of his ill-fitting shoes.

They skirted moonlit clearings where the risk of exposure was greatest, opting instead for the dense embrace of the forest. Branches snagged at their clothes, thorns tore at their flesh, leaving behind fabric and blood as unwilling tributes to the wilderness. Jacques winced as a bramble etched a stinging line across his cheek, but he dared not make a sound.

After ten kilometres of silent trudging, the noise of the River Bidassoa beckoned; a serpentine barrier in the night. Here, the water's murmur became a hushed roar, a tumultuous rush that sought to cleanse away their traces. Jacques hesitated at the bank, calculating the risk whilst undressing.

One by one they waded in, possessions held aloft.

The cold mountain water took each man's breath away as he ventured across – chest height at its deepest and perpetually pulling at their legs to wash them downstream and into the blackness. Jacques clutched the concealed map amidst a bundle of clothes, held high above his head in an attempt to keep them dry, shielding his precious items from the relentless grasp of the water.

"Quickly," Florentino hissed, his eyes reflecting a blend of moonlight and resolve.

On the far side, they scrambled up the ravine, a precarious ascent that betrayed their presence with skittering stones and laboured breaths. A few hundred metres to their left, sentry spotlights swept the landscape like lighthouse beams seeking ships in the storm. Jacques flattened himself against the earthy bank, his body moulding to the land as car headlights prowled the road above.

"Move," came the whispered command, and they pushed onwards, threading between pools of light and darkness. Scrambling up the jagged steep rocks of the ravine on the Spanish side, each of them postponing the celebration of crossing the border for later. With many kilometres yet to travel, the small band of escapees still experiencing waves of fear and freedom.

The first light of dawn broke over the horizon, casting a soft golden glow across the undulating fields. Florentino was a silhouette against the awakening sky, his posture unyielding and strong despite the hours they had trekked. Jacques, George and Arthur kept pace as best they could, their senses heightened to the slightest rustle in the hedgerows that bordered their path.

Every shadow threatened to morph into the uniformed figure of a carabinero; every distant sound a potential patrol.

They navigated the terrain with a blend of urgency and caution, an intricate dance with danger as their silent partner. The scent of dew-soaked grass filled Jacques' nostrils, mingling with the sharp tang of sweat. His jacket, a makeshift vault for the precious map, felt a little lighter – Spain was a big step closer to England.

At last, the farmhouse materialised like a mirage at the edge of their vision, its weather-beaten walls promising sanctuary. They crossed the threshold of safety just as the sky blushed with the hues of sunrise. Inside, the air was warm, rich with the aroma of frying onions and potatoes. A robust, aproned Spanish woman bustled around the hearth, ladling steaming milk into bowls and sliding generous wedges of tortilla onto cracked plates. Her smile was motherly, her movements efficient, offering them sustenance and comfort without sparing words.

Jacques sipped the hot milk, feeling it scald down his throat, a balm to his chilled bones. George and Arthur exchanged weary grins, their spirits buoyed by the simple fare and the hospitality of a stranger in a war-torn land.

"*Gracias*," Jacques murmured, his voice hoarse with fatigue, a silent prayer of deep gratitude woven into a single word.

The day unfolded like a dream as they rested and healed. Cuts were cleaned and bandaged, blisters treated with care. Laughter bubbled up between them, rare and precious – a shared reprieve from the constant terror that stalked their journey. They spoke of the future, of Blighty, and the lives they yearned to return to, allowing the warmth of camaraderie to eclipse the shadow of war, if only for a moment.

Night cloaked the sky in indigo when the British Consulate car pulled smoothly into the farmyard — silent, discreet, the culmination of their odyssey. Tension wound itself around Jacques' heart as the vehicle crept through the gates, headlamps extinguished. The driver stepped out, a whisper of movement in the darkness, his presence an echo of classified operations.

"All clear," he breathed, his voice barely audible as he surveyed the perimeter.

Inside, the walls pressed close with expectation. Jacques, George and Arthur emerged from the cocoon of the farmhouse, stepping into the cool embrace of the night. Their eyes met, each reflecting the same cocktail of anticipation and anxiety — the potent thrill of escape, so near they could taste its sweet promise on their tongues.

"Let's get you home," the driver said in a crisp English accent, his tone resolute, the phrase a talisman against the uncertainty that lay ahead.

Jacques clutched his jacket tighter, the map within a silent vow to continue the fight, to honour the sacrifices made along the way. Tonight, they would chase freedom south to Madrid, under the cover of darkness.

The car's passenger door creaked open, severing the night's silence as a second man emerged from the shadows. He was austere, his beige suit was spotless and the creases crisp, which jarred with the rural surroundings of their meeting.

"Mr Dumont." He addressed Jacques, his British accent slicing through the hushed whispers of the Spanish countryside. "I'm here on behalf of His Majesty's government."

Jacques' heart thrummed in his chest, a taut drumbeat of anticipation. The British attaché scanned the trio with a practised eye before delivering a gut punch disguised as protocol.

"Regrettably, Dumont, I've only room for two – your comrades, the airmen George and Arthur." His voice was matter-of-fact, devoid of empathy. "As a Belgian national, you fall outside the scope of our current operations, and these two gentlemen are needed back up in the sky to give the Luftwaffe a sound thrashing – sorry, old chap."

Protest clawed its way up Jacques' throat, words tangled in disbelief and an unyielding sense of injustice. But the attaché's expression remained unmoved, as impenetrable as the darkened windows of the diplomatic vehicle behind him.

Arthur slid into the hidden cavity beneath the rear seats while George disappeared under a musty blanket in the trunk. "Take care, *mon ami*," George added affectionately.

Trying to force these diplomats was pointless – after all, he processed, this was a military escape line and he had little right to be here.

Jacques pressed the heels of his hands into his eye sockets to alleviate the frustration, and the car rumbled away into the night. Alone. After spending so many days in the friendship of comrades, Lily, George, Arthur and the rest, the cold bite of abandonment cut deep.

Back at the farmhouse, Africa returned. The parasites in his blood wound through his veins, igniting a fever. Vivid images danced before his eyes: Ana's loving gaze, Kamia's innocent laughter – a tapestry of memories woven with pain and love.

He drifted between worlds, wails of African lament mingling with the echoing cries of Congolese wildlife. A vision of Kamia, radiant and ethereal, arms outstretched for a cuddle, her small hand almost tangible through the haze of his delirium.

Restez fort, *Papa. Stay strong,* she seemed to say, her blue eyes alight with an otherworldly glow.

The farmer, a caring observer amidst the chaos of Jacques' malaria, ushered him into the solace of the attic. There, nestled under the eaves, Jacques lay convalescing as days bled into nights. The farmer's weathered hands brought sustenance and chloroquine, each pill a lifeline pulling Jacques back from the precipice.

In the stillness of the attic, with the distant echo of war muffled by thick wooden beams, Jacques found himself suspended between despair and determination. The map pressed against his side – a constant reminder of the mission that he would never abort.

A few days later, Jacques Dumont gazed out from behind a newspaper, seated in a café on the bustling main square of San Sebastián, another city heavy with the shadow of occupation. Behind the posture and appearance of an unassuming Basque, his blue eyes were sharp, darting up only to scrutinise the faces that streamed past. Each person was a puzzle piece in a game of survival; each uniform a potential endgame. He sipped his coffee slowly, letting the bitter warmth slide down his throat, a stark contrast to the cool calculation in his mind.

The rucksack at his feet contained little more than provisions and the clothes on his back bore the wear of his journey, but Jacques carried something far more valuable – acute observation skills honed in the belly of resistance. As military patrols weaved through the crowd like predators stalking prey, he remained a ghost amongst the living, invisible yet vigilant.

His attention snagged on a man – a local by the look of him – whose eyes held a spark that spoke of defiance rather than submission. Jacques noticed his black trousers marked with the familiar white prints of flour. When the man turned into the bakery, Jacques folded his newspaper with deliberate calmness and followed, vaguely hoping that, if nothing else, he could plead solidarity amongst bakers.

Inside, the warm scent of fresh bread enveloped him, a comforting reminiscence of his days as the Ostend baker. He feigned interest in the delicious pastries displayed before him, all the while listening intently to the conversation between a customer and the proprietor. The coded lilt of their conversation was a language Jacques understood well.

"*Une demi baguette, s'il vous plaît,*" Jacques requested as the other customer sauntered out, leaving him alone with the baker. His voice was low, almost drowned out by the hum of the oven. He leaned in closer, his words a breathy whisper tinged with urgency and a conspiratorial glance. "I'm intrigued to know, sir … Are you able to help me with a matter of personal importance?"

The baker met his eyes, a flicker of understanding passing between them. "Meet me at the back, midnight," he replied, his tone casual but his message clear.

Back at the café table, the sky darkened and the square slowly emptied, the chill of the evening air seeping into Jacques' bones. With every tick of the clock, his thoughts churned, a whirlpool of suspicion and necessity. Could he trust this baker? It was a gamble with stakes higher than any loaf of bread or pastry could convey. But Jacques had walked the tightrope of trust many times before; it was a currency he knew how to spend.

As night veiled San Sebastián, Jacques felt the weight of solitude press against him. Doubt nipped at the fringes of his resolve, but there was a steel within him, the sort of conviction one has when there's only one option on the table. There was no choice but to move forward, to take the chance. Because for men like Jacques Dumont, caught in the gears of a world at war, trust was not a luxury – it was a leap into the unknown.

The potholed streets were slick with the evening's earlier rain, a sheen that reflected the moon's pale gaze as it peeked through the clouds. Jacques Dumont's shadow blended with the darkened alleyway where he stood watch, his eyes and ears never ceasing their vigilant sweep across the rear of the bakery. The hour was inching closer to midnight and his pulse tapped an anxious rhythm against his wrist, each passer-by, each whisper of movement in the periphery, shredding his nerves.

An hour had passed – a meticulous, painstaking hour of observation – and Jacques felt certain no German boots would tread upon this ground tonight. Yet, the certainty did nothing to calm him as the time for his meeting approached.

With the bell tower's chiming, Jacques approached the rear door of the bakery. A quiet knock, barely audible above the heartbeat in his ears, was his only announcement. Moments later it swung open, revealing the baker, who ushered him inside with a nod that seemed too casual for the gravity of their meeting.

"Come, come," the baker said, gesturing towards a table where two glasses and a bottle of cognac awaited them. "A drink to warm your night?"

Jacques accepted the glass but let it linger untouched in his hand. The room was sparse, the air heavy with the scent of yeast and flour, and the tension that rolled off the baker in invisible waves.

"Your questions earlier today," the baker began, pouring himself a generous measure of cognac. "You're seeking passage to England, yes?"

Jacques' blue eyes held the baker's gaze, searching for any signs of deceit. He knew better than to lay bare his intentions without first reading the man's allegiances. "Perhaps," he replied, the word wrapped in caution. "Can such arrangements be made?"

"Everything can be arranged ... for the right price," the baker replied, his voice low and probing. His eyes narrowed slightly, scrutinising Jacques' reaction.

It was then, in a rush of hubris, that Jacques decided to admit the risk. "Yes ... I need to stow away on a boat to England," he said, his voice a whisper of determination.

No sooner had the words left his lips than the baker's fist thumped twice upon the wooden tabletop. It was sudden, a signal that left no room for doubt, and before Jacques could react, the door burst open. Spanish Guardia Civil officers stormed the room, their faces grim and resolute under their green caps.

The baker stood up, a smug twist to his lips as he received a wad of pesetas from the officer leading the ambush. Betrayal … a palpable fog that clouded Jacques' thoughts and quickened his breath.

"*Manos arriba*!" The command was sharp, and Jacques was forced to his feet as handcuffs clicked around his wrists.

"Hey, sorry, amigo … no hard feelings!" the baker sneered, sinking both glasses of cognac to celebrate the night's work. Jacques met his gaze, the blue of his eyes icy with the betrayal.

"You piece of shit traitor," spat Jacques.

His battered espadrilles made no sound as Jacques was shuffled, quietly and without any fuss, away from the bakery by his captors. He would play the compliance game for now, but within him, the resolve to resist, to survive, remained unbroken.

Chapter 8:
The Highs and Lows of Miranda –
1942 (Jacques, aged 27)

Jacques' face remained an impassive mask as he sat across from the disinterested Spanish official. The humid, cramped interrogation room, reeking of stale cigarettes and fetid sweat-stench provided all the motivation Jacques needed to deliver a convincing performance of his alibi and get the hell out of there, sharpish. Papers rustled as the officer in charge glanced over Jacques' forged documents with a perfunctory squint.

"Jean-Pierre Bertillon," the officer mumbled, more to himself than to Jacques. "A lecturer in African studies from the Université de Liège?"

"Indeed," Jacques responded smoothly, his accent impeccably Belgian. "I am en route to Oxford University to continue my series of lectures. There has been a regrettable mix-up, I assure you."

"Swahili," the officer quipped sarcastically, looking up to catch any sign of fraud. "It says here you are fluent." More sarcasm.

"*Ndio, ninaweza kuzungumza Kiswahili,*" Jacques replied without missing a beat, the African syllables rolling off his tongue with ease. That touch of exotic knowledge seemed to cement his story in the officer's mind, like the final piece of a jigsaw puzzle impressively slipping into place.

"Very well, Mr Bertillon." The officer sighed, convinced, pushing the papers aside. "We have no interest in handing academics over to our friends in the Gestapo. You will be kept in our protection for now."

Jacques masked a sigh of relief with a curt nod, collecting his documents. As he was ushered out of the room, he allowed himself a smirk of triumph. The shambles of the Spanish administration had swallowed his tale whole.

Minutes turned into hours as Jacques, now just another body amongst many, shuffled onto a decrepit train bound for Miranda de Ebro. He found himself shoulder to shoulder with despairing souls – Polish soldiers whose eyes spoke of battles lost and Hungarian Jews who clutched their remnants of belongings with white-knuckled grips and scared expressions. The collective sense of group anxiety was palpable ... where were they going and exactly how bad would it be?

The train rattled violently on the tracks, its iron wheels screeching a litany of torment that seemed to resonate with each prisoner's emotional state. Jacques stared out through the barred windows at the passing countryside, his mind racing with thoughts of escape and survival.

As the imposing gates of Miranda de Ebro loomed into view, a fortress designed to crush hope beneath its shadow, Jacques steeled himself. Whatever lay ahead within those treacherous fences, he knew one thing for certain: his resolve to find Kamia and reach the shores of England was not dimmed – it was set ablaze. He would not let this place break him.

The sweaty grip of the prison guard's hands were impersonal as they frisked Jacques. Each pat-down was a potential discovery; each touch could reveal the concealed map that was his lifeline to freedom. Holding his breath, Jacques felt the coarse fabric of his jacket yield under searching fingers, but by some miracle, the map remained undiscovered.

"Name?" The prison guard's voice was devoid of interest.

"Jean-Pierre Bertillon," Jacques responded, his accent carefully neutral, betraying none of the concern clawing at his insides.

"French, then. You'll bunk with the others." The prison guard gestured dismissively towards a grizzled *cabo*, a burly supervisor clearly comfortable with violence, who looked Jacques up and down with predatory eyes.

"Come," the *cabo* grunted, leading Jacques through the maze of wooden barracks that reeked of despair and human filth. The bunk assigned to him was nothing more than a harsh slab of wood shared with three other hollow-eyed prisoners. The *cabo* watched as Jacques handed over his personal effects (including the precious jacket) for "safekeeping"- in the storeroom, and changed into thin homogeneously grey woollen prison jacket and trousers.

As Jacques lay on the unforgiving surface that night, pressed between strangers, he battled waves of claustrophobia and panic.

The window frame cast its shadow across his body like the crosshairs of a sniper's rifle. His thoughts twisted back to Africa, to the open savannahs of the Congo that now seemed like a distant dream. Here, there was no horizon – only the oppressive weight of captivity. He slept fleetingly and woke with backache.

Each day in Miranda de Ebro was a grotesque parody of life. At dawn, their slumber was shattered by the piercing call to "*bandera*", where they were herded like cattle to salute the very flag that symbolised their oppression. "Aviva Franco, Aviva España" – the words were a bitter poison on Jacques' tongue, but he shouted them through gritted teeth alongside the rest, arms aloft, muscles taut with disgust.

Labour in the nearby quarry was soul-breaking, an endless cycle of smashing and hauling stones that chipped away at both flesh and spirit. The guards watched them with shark-black eyes, quick to lash out with whips and batons at any sign of faltering. Despite his charismatic veneer, the relentless brutality threatened to crush Jacques' resolve.

Amongst the inmates, the Spanish were treated with particular harshness, their plight wrenching at Jacques' empathy. How could a country treat its own people so badly? He witnessed men, once proud and strong, reduced to scavenging husks, foraging through refuse for scraps to sustain their waning bodies. The suffering was a stark reminder of the harrowing depths to which humanity could sink.

Hope flickered dimly when the Polish inmates initiated a hunger strike; a desperate plea for mercy. As days passed without food, weakness became their shared language. Jacques felt his own strength ebbing away, yet he clung to the faint promise of change. When the strike finally bore fruit, it was not a victory but merely a reprieve from their torment – a few extra rations that did little to alleviate their gnawing hunger.

In those moments of quiet defiance, Jacques' mind would drift to Kamia dancing around their lounge back in Congo. The fire within him refused to be extinguished, fanned by each injustice endured, each indignity suffered. It was this unyielding flame that kept him alive, that fuelled his determination to survive the camp, to breathe free air once more, and to honour the silent vow he'd made to Ana, whose memory sustained him through the darkest hours.

Jacques' hands grew calloused, his muscles ached from the relentless toil, yet he never allowed despair to get the better of him. The quarry's gruelling labour reminded him of childhood – of the dense Congo jungles where resilience was not just a trait but a necessity for survival. He had learned early to find solace in small victories, to grasp tightly onto fleeting moments of joy amidst adversity. His thoughts always clung to Kamia, her image a beacon guiding him through the haze of exhaustion. Jacques constantly reminded himself that jungle life had trained him for this – he had survived that … and now he would survive this.

"¡Levántalo!" the cabo barked, snapping Jacques back to reality as they hoisted another basket of stones, stepping over the lifeless casualty of this morning's endeavour to return from loading the baskets to wielding mallets. Even though they were in the open air, the quarry wreaked of death.

"Never let them win, Dumont," he murmured to himself, a private rebellion against the crushing weight of hopelessness that encouraged everyone to lie down, to give up. His stubbornness became his strength, a subtle defiance that bewildered his captors and inspired his fellow prisoners.

One afternoon, as they shuffled home from stone-breaking, barely bothering to look at the pile of decaying skeletal corpses stacked up beside the road, Jacques caught the eye of the *cabo*, offering a weary yet genuine grin.

"In my previous life, I was a baker," he shared, his Belgian-French accent tinged with pride. "I could knead dough with more vigour than we carry these rocks."

The *cabo*, a hulking figure hardened by the brutalities of war, paused, eyeing Jacques curiously. Over the following days, Jacques regaled him with tales of golden loaves and sweet pastries, each story deliberately woven with warmth and nostalgia. It wasn't long before the *cabo*, surprisingly charmed, arranged for Jacques to be reassigned to the prison bakery.

The task was no less arduous, but it brought Jacques closer to the essence of who he once was. Under his skilled hands, the bread began to transform. Even with subpar ingredients, each loaf boasted a better texture, a more palatable taste.

Word of the remarkable improvement in the daily bread reached the stomach of the senior camp commander, whose curiosity had been piqued. A summons arrived, and one afternoon Jacques found himself standing in the commandant's office. Observant as ever, Jacques saw before him a rather slight, scrawny man whose uniform was so clean that Jacques concluded he had never been close to actual war.

"Are you the new baker?" the commandant inquired in Spanish, scrutinising Jacques.

"Yes, sir. Jean-Pierre Bertillon, at your service, Commandant." Jacques responded respectfully in Spanish. "I was taught to bake as a boy, growing up in the Belgian Congo, and my father was a baker in Bruges, sir," he lied.

To commemorate their meeting, Jacques had crafted a loaf unlike any other – a tribute to Spain, with the Eagle of St John emblazoned across the crust, a motif used by Franco's supporters. It was audacious, perhaps foolishly so, but Jacques had always played by different rules.

"Remarkable," the commandant admitted, a rare flicker of appreciation in his stern gaze. "But can you make bread this good every day?"

"Give me quality flour and proper ingredients, and I will ensure that the officers' breakfast is unmatched," Jacques said confidently, his voice carrying the subtle cadence of someone accustomed to luxury.

"Very well," the commandant agreed after a moment's contemplation. "You will have what you need. And if you require assistance ..."

"Three apprentice bakers would be most beneficial, sir."

"Granted. But remember, your bread better remain exceptional or you risk punishment."

"Of course, Commandant," Jacques said, the hint of a smile in his eyes.

Back in the bakery, Jacques worked the ovens with a renewed fervour, the scent of baking bread mingling with dreams of freedom. Each loaf was a step closer to England, to Kamia, and to the end of this nightmare. In the swelter of the kitchen, amidst sacks of flour and the cries of distant suffering, Jacques Dumont, once a mere captive, began to forge his path towards liberation.

Jacques' hands moved deftly, shaping the dough with practised ease as the warmth from the ovens fought back the chill of a Spanish winter. The bakery, a sanctuary of heat and the rich aroma of bread, stood in sharp contrast to the grim reality outside its walls. The officers came for their fresh loaves, offering nods of approval at the quality, never suspecting the eyes that watched them, weighed their character, searched for weakness.

"*Excellente*," one officer remarked, breaking off a piece of the steaming bread.

"*Gracias*," Jacques replied with an easy smile, while his mind raced with calculations. Each officer befriended was another potential ally, or at least a lesser threat in his grand scheme of survival and escape.

In this camp, where life hung by a thread, Jacques had carved out a niche of relative safety. He protected the sickest prisoners by drawing them into the bakery's fold as his trainees, assigning tasks within their waning strength to keep them from the clutches of the death squads. The scent of baking bread served as a thin veil over the stench of desperation that seeped through the camp.

But even here, among the sacks of flour and the rhythmic pulse of kneading, starvation gnawed at every soul. The rations were meagre – sawdust bulked out the bread meant for the common prisoner, making it barely edible. Tempers flared in camp, brother turned against brother, all for a morsel to stave off hunger's relentless advance.

Jacques, ever resourceful, stretched the provisions, added water where he could, and offered crumbs of comfort to those whose spirits were most frayed. Each act of kindness was a silent rebellion against the cruelty that sought to strip them of their humanity.

Months passed, and Jacques worked his plan with meticulous care. Every delivery day, he secreted away handfuls of flour beneath a loose floor tile. As the night before Passover approached, the opportunity to give hope began.

Evening fell on the 18th of April 1943, and the camp descended into the usual tense quietude. Under the cover of darkness, Jacques slipped into the bakery. His heart pounded in sync with the distant, vigilant footsteps of patrolling guards. Kneading the stolen flour with skill and haste, he remembered Maman Nzeza – memories from a world so far removed from this place of barbed wires and watchtowers.

The dough took form as a special seder bread, simple yet profound in its significance. This would be their Passover matzah, the sustenance of faith on a night that commemorated liberation for Jews across the world. With the mixture ready, Jacques crept towards the block housing the Jewish prisoners, each step a defiance of the searchlights' sweeping gaze.

A soft knock, a barracks door creaking open, the rabbi's face registering surprise at the sight of Jacques holding the precious dough. Words were unnecessary as tears filled the old man's eyes, an understanding passing between them in the silence. Jacques looked past the old man to the hollow, gaunt faces beyond. Holy bread for holy people enduring this unholiest of places.

Minutes later, the small potbelly stove glowed red, and the flat unleavened matzah baked on top to a humble perfection. Amidst whispered prayers, the Jewish prisoners broke bread together, their faces alight with a hope that transcended their emaciated bodies.

Jacques melted back into the shadows, relishing the taste. Hope was indeed more nourishing than bread; it fortified the spirit against the gradual erosion of body and mind.

As he opened the door to his own barracks, it gave a slight creak that broke the silence of the squalid room. Jacques' heart pounded in his chest as he slid into the shadows, hoping to dissolve into the darkness and not wake any of his fellow prisoners.

But the *cabo*, a silhouette against the dim lantern light, was waiting.

"Where have you been, Bertillon?" the *cabo*'s voice growled, deep and dangerous.

"I was checking the ovens," Jacques replied, his voice steady despite the adrenaline coursing through his veins.

"You lying Belgian swine." The accusation came swift, the *cabo*'s eyes glinting with a mix of suspicion and contempt. "There is no warmth in your story."

Before Jacques could protest, rough hands grabbed him, dragging him into the light. A fist collided with his stomach, folding him in half, the air rushing from his lungs. Another blow struck his face, sending stars exploding across his vision. Pain splintered through his body as he crumpled to the floor.

"Curfew is curfew," the *cabo* spat, his boot finding Jacques' ribs with a sickening crunch.

Lying on the ground, each breath a twinge of agony, Jacques clung to consciousness. He had to survive: for Kamia.

Dawn broke with a cold indifference. Jacques dragged himself upright, every movement an ordeal. His face was a mask of bruises, the purple hues stark against his pallid skin. His right eye was swollen shut. Limping towards the bakery, a broken body held together by sheer willpower.

Inside, the scent of baking bread was a cruel mockery today. Jacques set about his tasks, kneading dough with trembling hands, his injuries hidden beneath the baker's apron but impossible to forget.

The camp commandant entered, uniform pristine in the morning light. His gaze fell upon Jacques, taking in his battered, swollen face. For a moment, there was a flicker of something human in the commandant's eyes.

"Sir, please may I request my jacket for a little comfort on my beaten body?" Jacques chanced, his voice a rasp.

Surprisingly, the commandant nodded. "Very well, Bertillon. You make the best bread in this godforsaken place."

With that rare nod of compassion, Jacques felt a surge of relief. The jacket meant more than warmth – it was the key to his freedom; the map sewn into its lining, his lifeline.

Within an hour the worn, faded leather jacket was returned to him. Jacques' fingers brushed over the fabric, feeling the outline of his salvation. He would bear the beatings, the torment, and the hunger. For within the threads of that leather coat lay the path to liberation, and he would follow it to the very end.

Dawn's first light crept into the bakery as Jacques Dumont pressed a crusty loaf of bread into the hands of the flour delivery driver – a silent message concealed within its hollowed heart. The man nodded with a feigned nonchalance, tucking the bread under his arm as he prepared to leave the confines of Miranda de Ebro.

"British Consul … Madrid," Jacques whispered, the urgency in his voice belying the casual exchange. "Extra food … release for prisoners."

"Understood," the driver muttered, casting a wary glance at the shadows that danced just beyond the reach of the dim bakery lights.

With the truck rumbling away into the distance, Jacques turned back to the warmth of the ovens, a deceptive calm settling over him. But the peace was short-lived. Within hours, the camp was alight with tension, a storm brewing within the barracks.

"Someone here is communicating with the outside world!" The prison guard's voice boomed across the compound, piercing through the morning roll-call like a bullet. The prisoners were rounded up like cattle, each man's face etched with fear and fatigue.

"Who sent the message?" the officer demanded, eyes scanning the sea of emaciated faces before him. Silence hung heavy in the air; not a soul dared to betray Jacques, their unspoken solidarity a fortress against the interrogator's wrath.

The consequence was swift – a double shift of hard labour, moving stones until muscles screamed and spirits waned. Yet through it all, Jacques stood tall among them, his gratitude radiating in silent nods and touches of camaraderie. The shared suffering only forged a stronger bond, each man's resolve steeling against the oppressors. But more died on that double shift than any other day in the camp – 12 hours of hard labour consumed the last strength of many. Jacques never did wash the blood from his hands, for the rest of his life, grateful for their secrecy.

***

As the months passed, the prisoners of Miranda de Ebro grew familiar with the routines. Death became routine also. Clearing out the dead bodies every morning from the dorms was just another job, devoid of the luxury of love afforded by ceremony and ritual in peacetime.

One routine that put everyone on edge was the monthly visit from the Gestapo intelligence officers. Once summoned into their "office" it was unlikely that you would see your comrades again – prisoners simply vanished.

And so it was that one spring morning the name of Jean-Pierre Bertillon was called loud and clear from the parade ground to line up with three others against the wall of the "inspection" block located just inside the front entrance of the camp, far away from the dorms. Jacques had the good sense to slip off his jacket and give it to Witek, the Polish politician and friend standing beside him, before making his way forward.

The four anxious prisoners lined up with their backs to the wall of the interrogation block, as the pleasant sunshine silhouetted their emaciated limbs onto the concrete wall behind them, and awaited their fate. Jacques focused on breathing deeply, playing his alias story over and over in his mind. He remembered fondly the time spent with Lily, as she coached him on what to say and how to act. He wished he had listened better, rather than wistfully recollecting the passionate love they had made the night before, the softness of her body writhing on his.

Bertillon was the first, led into the menacing gloom and coolness of the soundproof inspection building.

There were no windows – just walls and foreboding as Jacques was shoved in, handcuffed. Two Gestapo agents nonchalantly sat smoking behind a rusty metal table. They beckoned him to sit at the lone metal chair opposite. The guard attached one of Jacques' cuffs to the chair and ambled out, locking the door behind him.

Jacques instantly began reading the ominous characters before him. One was a giant – easily six foot four, with a thick neck, bald perspiring head and perfectly trimmed beard. The other, a rat. Small and slight, small round spectacles balanced on a pale taut face. Both had hung their characteristic black leather trench coats on hooks protruding from the wall, military caps on top displaying the feared eagle emblem. Their military uniform was impeccable, a ballroom sheen to their boots. Resting on the floor beside the rat's foot was a worn leather doctor's bag.

"Tell us about the baking." They immediately cut to the chase in German. Jacques could see this freight train coming a mile away.

"I learned it in the Congo." Jacques chose to reply in French, and would only give them the smallest crumbs.

The wiry Gestapo officer switched to flawless French. "The commandant says you bake the best prison bread west of Ostend." They paused to examine his face for a twitch, a look, a gesture … anything that registered guilt or fear.

Nothing.

"Well … that's very kind of the commandant … but really, I just learned it from a Congolese grandmother in a village outside Léopoldville."

"Well, we have a problem then, don't we … because you look like someone we would be very interested in locating. A baker. He took something of ours and we want it back."

"I don't know how to help you, sir."

The thin one stood and leaned in menacingly close to Jacques' face.

They could smell the stench of each others' breath.

Jacques matched his gaze, desperately hoping that his breathing rate wouldn't rise any further. This was the moment when all of the oppression from his past, all of the hatred from the missionary fathers, all of the racism against his loved ones, all of the colonial abuse, all of the imprisonment, and every German sneer … it all raged inside. Jacques could outstare this bully for days.

The officer spoke very slowly, enunciating so much that spittle landed on Jacques' face.

"I think you know exactly what we're looking for … Jacques Dumont."

"I'm sorry, sir, but you have the wrong person – I am Jean-Pierre Bertillon, and whilst I may know how to bake, I can assure you that I'm a lecturer in African studies from—"

"ENOUGH OF THESE LIES!!" the German screamed back, millimetres from his face.

Then … silence.

"You have choices, Jacques." A psychopathic calmness returned to the officer's voice as he settled back into his seat.

"You can tell us where the map is, and we send you back to the camp. Or ... my colleague will persuade you with pain and suffering until you beg me to listen."

"But I know nothing about a map ... or Ostend ... or this Dumont you mentioned. Please ... I'm just an academic."

It was a well delivered, very authentic plea. Jacques almost believed it himself. So good that the Gestapo man even began to wonder if this was indeed the thief. The dishevelled, malnourished wretch before him barely resembled the photo in his file.

But the torturing began, nevertheless.

The Gestapo brute took the pliers from the bag and tore a nail from Jacques' ring finger, sending pain, the likes of which Jacques had never experienced, shooting up his arm. Screams of agony came from deep within.

They hung Jacques by his handcuffs up onto one of the hooks embedded in the wall, his back to the wall, so that the blood dripped onto his face from the finger wound.

The wiry officer enjoyed placing a thin metal strip (a little larger than a credit card) into Jacques' mouth.

In an instant the brute took a run up and rammed his boot into Jacques' crotch. His mouth clamped hard around the metal strip slicing into the corners of his mouth and splitting his cheeks open, blood pouring from his mouth.

Multiple times the boot landed, pain searing through his pelvis, his testicles crushed.

Faced with insufferable and ongoing agony the human mind copes in strange ways. Jacques' mind was somewhere else now … it took him away to wander the Congolese jungle with his girls, listening to birdsong in the canopy, mesmerised by the shafts of light dappling the jungle floor … whilst the demons continued their work.

They messed him up so badly that Jacques was barely alive after their onslaught, let alone capable of answering questions.

Four camp guards were needed to remove his limp, bloodied, broken body from the room. It was only the chance intervention of the commandant, who witnessed Jacques being taken from the block, that diverted the guards towards the infirmary rather than depositing him on top of the pile of the previous night's deceased.

The camp doctors and staff did their best for Jacques. He was as well-liked as any prisoner could be … and maybe that meant he received a little extra morphine. One of the prisoners persuaded the nurse to take their blood, match it, and give a pint of it to Jacques.

In those first few days, as Jacques' brain swelled, he drifted in and out of consciousness. The light called him … he felt the deep love of Ana's presence … he wanted to be with her so badly, but something drew him back, into his broken carcass – and that something was Kamia.

It wasn't his time.

After a week, and although experiencing intense pain, at least Jacques was conscious and alive. He was also comforted to notice that his jacket was supporting his head, doubling as an extra pillow. He wept when the doctor confirmed that Jacques would never be able to father any children. He wept for himself, but mainly because he wanted nothing more than a cuddle from his baby girl in that moment, to make everything OK.

After three weeks of convalescing, thanks in no small part to an extra ration here and there, smuggled in by the infirmary inmates, Jacques felt strong enough to offer his bed to someone in greater need, and headed back into his bakery. There was precious little time to execute an escape plan before the Gestapo returned for their monthly visit.

After just a few days of secret conversations and scheming, the plan was ready.

Under the cloak of darkness and exhaustion, Jacques convened with his bakery apprentices — their faces gaunt, but eyes alight with a spark of defiance. One held the ladder as another pushed empty flour sacks into the eaves and joists of the bakery roof, hidden from view.

"Tomorrow," he instructed, his voice barely above a whisper, "when we load up the empties. Everyone clear?"

The plan was meticulous, each detail scrutinised and rehearsed in hushed tones. As the morning sun rose, the bakery was alive with nervous energy. The sack supposedly containing all of the residual beige burlap sacks actually cradled Jacques, his body contorting to fit within its canvas womb.

The truck reversed through the delivery gate at noon, flanked by armed guards.

"Move quickly," Jacques' closest ally urged, grimacing as he and another comrade swung the human-laden sack into the back of the truck with a thud. Another prisoner climbed up, using more strength than their thin arms could afford, and dragged Jacques up towards the cab, strapping him to the truck frame and checking the knot securing the sack above his head.

"May fortune favour you, my friend," another breathed, his gaze lingering on the sack that supposedly contained the empties.

The ruse was a razor's edge walk between freedom and catastrophe. Hearts thundered in unison as the driver, now complicit in their ploy, signed the paperwork. The guards, lulled by the monotony of their duties, were oblivious to the switch – their attention diverted by a feigned scuffle among the prisoners.

With every jolt of the truck, Jacques' heart leapt, his breath shallow in the stifling darkness of his floury enclosure. It was only when the truck ambled past the gates, the familiar luminescence of the camp fading into the background, that he allowed himself to believe.

Escape was within reach – every bump in the road a step closer to liberty, each turn a twist away from the demons. Cramped in the dusty package of his escape, Jacques afforded himself a half-smile.

The truck's engine hummed a lullaby of liberation as it snaked through the Spanish countryside. Jacques Dumont, concealed within the sanctuary of his flour sack, counted the seconds, each one drawing him closer to the precipice of escape. His muscles cramped from confinement, his body slick with perspiration that mingled with the dust of flour, he focused on the rhythm of the road – a code tapping out the promise of deliverance.

A sudden deceleration, then the soft crunch of gravel beneath tyres, signalled the moment. Time constricted like a noose. With an agility born of desperation, Jacques tore through the fabric of his enclosure using a screw stashed in his pocket, his movements precise. The truck slowed for a curve, and in the span of a heartbeat, he rolled out into the void, hitting the ground with a muffled thud that knocked the breath from his lungs and sent twinges of pain shooting through his pelvis. He lay motionless, heart pounding, as the vehicle continued its journey, oblivious to the weight it had shed.

Pushing himself up, Jacques crawled into the underbrush, the brambles scraping against his skin, the earth cool and damp beneath his hands. His every instinct screamed to run, but he tempered his zeal, allowing the shadows to swallow him whole. His freedom was palpable, a living thing pulsating with energy around him. He would bide his time until the cloak of night grew closer.

Hours passed, marked only by the slow wheel of stars overhead. Then, moving with the stealth of a panther, Jacques emerged from his natural camouflage. His stride was laboured, his path chosen with care to avoid the searching beams of any late-night patrols. The coast beckoned, its briny tang mingling with the cool breeze that caressed his face, whispering promises of new beginnings.

At last, the cove of a small fishing town came into view, with the Bay of Biscay stretching unmistakably beyond. The sun was just rising as the townsfolk began their daily routines. Jacques found a convenient bush positioned on a cliff overlooking the town from the east. After ditching the prison shirt and grey woollen jacket, wearing only the trousers, shoes and his trusty leather coat, Jacques settled down to observe people from this vantage point ... noting their business, their behaviour.

Hope began to dawn too. There were no Guardia Civil or Carabinero to be seen. And plenty of boats. Things were looking up in the mind of Groupe G's most notorious member. It was midday and Jacques couldn't wait any longer to make his move. Jacques noticed an old lady hobbling back towards her home with a basket of goods. He accentuated his side parting with a sweep of his hand (as if doing his hair would distract her from his skeletal appearance), smiled broadly, switched on maximum Dumont charm and made his approach.

***

After a hearty vegetable soup, and politely accepting the offer of some of her dead husband's clothes, Jacques left the dear old lady's home just before 11 pm. She blushed when Jacques kissed her on the cheek by way of thanks. Bobbing gently beside the jetty was his vessel to salvation – a simple-looking blue-painted fishing boat with a small cabin to house the captain and enough room for a few bodies to shelter. Jacques' approach was cautious, his sunken eyes scanning for signs of betrayal or trap. But there was none. Just the soft lap of waves against wooden hulls and the distant call of a gull.

"*Qui va là?*" a hushed voice challenged as he neared the water's edge.

"*Liberté*," Jacques replied, the code word slipping from his lips like a sacred vow.

"*Vite*, come aboard," came the response, a hand reaching out from the obscurity to pull him onto the deck.

His feet touched the wooden planks and he was ushered through the cabin and below deck, hidden away once more, but this time in the company of comrades. The boat lurched forward, deftly slipping its moorings and chugging softly into the dark silky sea, with only the winking guidance of celestial navigators. As the coastline receded, becoming nothing more than a soft haze on the horizon, Jacques allowed himself a small, triumphant smile.

The aches from his earlier tumble into the ditch paled in comparison to the sense of relief that surged through his veins. He felt each bruise and swelling as a badge of honour – a testament to his resolve. The hardships of the camp, the torture and death he had witnessed, they were chapters of a past life, disappearing behind him with each nautical mile.

As dawn broke the next morning, spilling gold over the waters, Jacques peered out through the open cabin windows, holding a mug of hot steaming tea and sensing the sun's warmth on his cheeks. The soft sea breeze carried with it the promise of freedom as England awaited, a distant haven inching closer with each push of the tide. His journey was far from over, but another step towards slaying the oppressor, and locating Kamia, had been taken.

Chapter 9:

Escape to Blighty – Late 1942
(Jacques, aged 27)

The murky green waves of the English Channel chopped against the hull of the fishing boat, a rhythmic thud that had become both comfort and curse during the perilous journey from the north coast of Spain. For more than 40 hours this inconspicuous little boat had somehow evaded the U-boats and mines that littered the Bay of Biscay, for which Captain Lucien and his precious cargo regularly whispered prayers and gratitude to the Divine.

Jacques Dumont, his blond hair plastered to his forehead with salt spray, stood resolutely at the bow, his piercing blue eyes fixed on the horizon where the Isle of Wight emerged like a sliver of hope against the dawn sky.

"Royal Navy patrol," Lucien De Smet's gruff voice called out from behind the wheel. The captain's words sent a current of anticipation through the weary passengers huddled in the boat's belly, their fates now a hair's breadth from turning.

As the patrol boat drew near, its sleek grey hull cutting through the water with authoritative ease, Jacques felt trepidation. This was it — the moment of surrender, the end of their flight. The Royal Navy vessel signalled them to cut the engines. De Smet complied, the abrupt silence falling heavy around them.

"Hands where we can see them!" a voice boomed across the water as the navy boat, bristling with guns, sidled up alongside the fishing vessel. Armed marines in crisp uniforms peered down, rifles trained on the escapees. Jacques raised his hands high, his gaze catching on the British white ensign fluttering proudly on the aft flagpole. *No heroics*, he reminded himself, despite the guns pointed at him.

"Prepare to be boarded," came the next command, and soon enough, the clank of boots on deck signalled their compliance. Jacques felt the cold metal of handcuffs click around his wrists, biting into the pre-existing lacerations — a precautionary measure, he understood, but one that chafed against his skin and pride alike.

The evacuees were herded onto the patrol boat, which then escorted them towards Portsmouth. Jacques squinted against the sunlight glinting off the water, every mile closer to shore loosening another knot of tension within him. Another troop of marines awaited them at the docks, their presence an intimidating welcome, rifles at the ready.

"Move along," they ordered, guiding the group off the boat and onto trucks that would take them for questioning. Jacques stumbled slightly on the solid ground; his legs unsteady after two days at sea. The handcuffs rattled – an incongruous sound amidst the muted shuffle of feet and subdued murmurs of his companions.

Yet, as the truck rumbled away from the docks, a profound sense of relief washed over Jacques. His eyes welled up, tears carving clean lines through the salty grime on his face. He let them fall, the joy of safety overwhelming after the incessant undercurrent of fear that had gripped him for so long.

"Thank you," he whispered in English, the words more prayer than statement. The language felt familiar on his tongue, a testament to the time spent with George and Arthur, and practised with the British prisoners in Miranda de Ebro. Those lessons, shared in whispers and etched into his memory, were now a lifeline in this new chapter of his life.

"Quiet back there!" a marine barked, mistaking his gratitude for insubordination.

Jacques only smiled through his tears, nodding his acquiescence. This was England; this was freedom. And for the first time in what felt like an eternity, he allowed himself to believe that perhaps, just perhaps, there might be a chance at a future unfettered by war's cruel grasp.

Jacques' heart raced as the MI6 interrogator, a stoic man with a clipped moustache and sharp eyes, slid the map across the table. The stale air of the dimly lit room was thick with tension. Jacques' hands were clammy as he reached out, his fingertips brushing the delicate paper edges.

"Where did you get this?" The officer's voice was cold, precise; the embodiment of controlled suspicion.

"It was given to me ... by a friend," Jacques lied, his voice steady despite the turmoil churning within him. He had not anticipated the gravity the map would carry, nor the dire consequences of its possession. Why admit to stealing the map, giving the interrogator the impression that he was some sort of criminal? he concluded.

"Given? Or stolen, Mr Dumont? This is highly sensitive material, and quite frankly it screams espionage."

"Please," Jacques implored, his eyes locking onto the officer's for maximum sincerity, "you must believe me. I am no spy. I worked with the Comet Line, with Lily – Elise Vignol. She entrusted me with it."

The interrogator leaned back, scepticism etched into his furrowed brow. "Lily, eh? Let's see if your story holds water."

Days dragged on in Chatham Military Prison, the weight of uncertainty bearing down on Jacques like shackles. He reminded himself that he had been in much worse prisons before. This cell was palatial compared to the Miranda camp ... he had access to books, and the three square meals a day tasted edible. Yet he felt little in the way of peace ... the relentless echo of being considered a German spy haunted his thoughts. Little did they know how much he hated them. To his mind, the only good German was a dead German.

Then, one bland morning, quite unexpectedly, the door opened and a new face appeared – a naval intelligence agent with a bounce in his step, a sharp sense of style, and a glint in his eye. Jacques liked the chap immediately.

"Mr Dumont, my name is Tom Duggleby and I work in Naval Intelligence. Let's have a chat, shall we?" The agent's tone carried the casual air of a gentleman discussing cricket scores rather than matters of national security.

Jacques recounted his tale once more, the words flowing with practised ease, yet laced with an undercurrent of desperation. He spoke of his work with the resistance, of the lives saved, and the irreparable bond formed with a woman whose courage knew no bounds. The suave agent listened intently, his expression unreadable, yet something in his gaze suggested a flicker of understanding.

"Alright, Mr Dumont," the agent said after a lengthy silence, "I'll verify your claims with MI9. But if you've lied ..."

"I haven't," Jacques interjected firmly. "You will find that everything I've told you is true."

True to his word, the agent departed, returning some days later with a confirmation that lifted the suffocating veil of doubt. "It seems you are indeed a friend of Lily's," he conceded, a trace of respect threading through his words. "Your assistance has been noted."

As quickly as the weight of suspicion had gathered over Jacques, it dissipated without fanfare. The map became a ghost, its existence alluded to only in whispered corridors and the briefest mention tucked away in a back column of the newspapers. Reports of naval victories over enemy U-boats trickled in, whispers of "important intelligence sources" bolstering the spirits of a nation at war.

Yet for Jacques, who had stared down the barrel of accusation and emerged unscathed, the map was a silent testament to the enduring struggle – a struggle that raged on beneath the surface of the sea and within the hearts of those bound by duty and honour.

A few short months later, and thanks to Tom pulling a few strings at the Admiralty Interview Board, Jacques Dumont's reflection in the polished brass porthole of *HMS Athelston* was one of a man reborn. He looked healthy, was finding it increasingly easy to laugh and joke with his shipmates, and modestly acknowledged that he looked the bee's knees in this crisp Royal Navy uniform. With every day that passed he was returning to something like his old self.

The rhythmic thrum of the engines and the salty tang of sea air had become his new normal, replacing the fear that once clung to him like a second skin. As he gazed at the rolling waves, and the brood of supply ships being escorted safely into port, the laughter and camaraderie of his shipmates echoed around him, a testament to the lifeblood of the vessel and the nation it served.

"Never pegged you for the brooding type," a voice jested from behind, as warm and inviting as the hand that clapped Jacques' shoulder. Tom, with his easy smile and eyes that sparkled with mischief, had become more than an ally: he was the brother Jacques had never had.

"Merely contemplating our next victory — not against Fritz — I mean with the girls at the dance next weekend," Jacques winked, his tone laced with the cheeky optimism that had wormed its way back into his heart.

"Ah, spoken like a true sailor! Speaking of which, we don't have to wait 'til next weekend — tonight we celebrate on terra firma. I know a spot in London that'll make you forget all about this floating tin can."

***

Although the enforced blackout shrouded the city streets, behind tightly veiled windows there was still the promise of merriment and forgetfulness. Jacques found himself amidst a blur of young people dancing as if the only thing that mattered was now, and the swing band synched with the newfound rhythm of freedom.

Enjoying Tom's company and sharing tales of life before the war over many martinis, it wasn't long before Jacques' gaze was sidetracked by beauty.

"Hey, Tom, angels at three o'clock ... what say we head over and say hello before the GIs arrive, eh?"

The two dapper military men slid into seats on the girls' table and began flashing their smiles and conversation. Jacques made no attempt to hide his attraction for Renée – whose laughter seemed to weave through the smoky air. And as fate would have it ... Renée happened to be Belgian too.

"Care for a dance with a dance-hall connoisseur?" he teased, extending his hand with a confident grin.

"Yes, I'll ask Tom," Renée quipped ironically, cutting Jacques down to size with a smile. "Go on then ... only if you promise not to step on my toes," she added, her bold voice betraying no hint of feminine meekness.

As they swayed and spun to the music, Jacques found himself entranced by her assertiveness, every word and movement exuding a vitality that could outshine the darkest past. They spoke of dreams and whispered of a future in Ostend, where peace would wash over the soft sand beach.

After a wonderful night of flirting and dancing, as Jacques' head touched the pillow back in Tom's spare room, Kamia's face flickered behind his eyelids.

Stepping off the early morning train to Chatham with a thumping headache, Jacques boarded *HMS Athelston*, grabbed a coffee and headed for the fresh air of the aft deck, his gaze hardened by resolve. He wanted to savour the warmth of Renée's company, the laughter they shared, and the hope that blossomed between them. Sure, she was totally gorgeous, and maybe one day they would find love, but Jacques couldn't shake off the cold embers of loss. There was only one conclusion. He must hide his woes from Renée – she wouldn't understand, and he risked losing her if she knew the whole truth about his past.

The taut silence of the Chatham naval intelligence office was a stark contrast to the pervasive hum of activity from the docks. Jacques' fingers drummed an anxious rhythm on the cold metal table, his eyes fixed on Tom's form hunched over scattered papers and photographs.

"Any word?" Jacques' voice cut through the stillness, tinged with a hint of desperation.

Tom exhaled slowly, the weight of his findings shadowing the lines of his face. "It's Wout De Vries ... he's been executed. The Nazis caught him after a failed sabotage attempt on a military supply train. Fritz had infiltrated the resistance group and De Vries was caught in the act."

"Are you sure there's no mistake?" Jacques' voice heaved with disappointment.

Tom's expression, usually so full of irrepressible humour, now bore a sombre cast. "I've confirmed it through three separate contacts," he replied grimly.

A chill suffused Jacques' body, as though ice water had replaced his blood. Wout – his last hope of finding Kamia – was gone. Dead. Jacques' vision blurred, the edges of reality fraying like old rope.

"Damn it!" He slammed his fist onto the table, a futile strike against fate itself.

Tom reached across, placing a steadying hand on Jacques' arm. "I'm sorry, old chap. I truly am."

Jacques stood, his movements mechanical, driven by a force beyond despair.

Later that rainy December afternoon, as the blackout of Chatham High Street was punctuated with the laughter of couples arm in arm, Jacques felt like an imposter in this scene of wartime merriment. He met Renée outside Cinema Rex, her face alight with anticipation, and the contrast between her joy and his internal desolation was palpable.

"Something's wrong," she said almost immediately, her perceptive gaze locking onto his. "Tell me."

In that moment, Jacques wanted nothing more than to pour out everything – the pain of Ana's loss, the ache for Kamia, the nightmares that haunted him. But fear gripped him, the fear of losing her – she was the silver lining in his life since the darkness of Miranda de Ebro.

"It's this damn war," he lied, forcing a smile that didn't reach his eyes. "Just ... just tired of it all, you know?"

Renée searched his face, her brow furrowed with concern. "We're all tired," she said softly, reaching out to squeeze his hand. "But there's more than fatigue in those eyes, Dumont."

"Let's just enjoy the film," Jacques deflected, desperate to escape the scrutiny, to bury the truth deep within himself. She nodded hesitantly, but her worry remained etched in the lines of her face.

"Damn," Renée cursed under her breath, her grip tightening on Jacques' arm. "I've left my umbrella in the post office."

Jacques stopped, concern etching his features. "I can go with you."

"No, no, you'll miss the newsreel," she insisted, pressing a cinema ticket into his hand. "You need this more than I do. Go on, I'll be right there." Her tone was assertive, as always.

With reluctance, Jacques nodded, the warm caress of her lips on his cheek, lingering as they parted. He turned away, the weight of the ticket heavy in his palm, each step towards the cinema entrance an effort to keep the shadows of his past at bay.

Meanwhile, Renée retraced her path with purposeful strides, her heels clicking rhythmically against the wet pavement. After a couple of minutes, Renée turned left off Chatham High Street into Whitaker Street and reached the post office just as another barrage of rain unleashed from the heavens. She grabbed the forgotten umbrella, its fabric a bright splash of red amidst the gloom.

And then, stepping back into the street, the world exploded.

A deafening roar shattered the air; the ground trembled with violent fury. A flash of searing light, then darkness, as if the night had devoured the day whole. The shockwave hit Renée like a physical blow, throwing her off her feet, the umbrella torn from her grasp.

Dazed, ears ringing, Renée lay sprawled on the pavement, her mind struggling to make sense of the chaos. Slowly, slowly, reality seeped back in — an alarm ringing in the distance, the acrid scent of smoke assaulting her nostrils. She pushed herself up, her hands scraping against the rough ground, her vision clearing to reveal the unthinkable.

Cinema Rex was gone.

Where moments ago stood a fine art deco building, now only a gaping hole remained, spewing dust and debris into the air. Flames licked the ruins, casting an eerie glow against the curtain of rain.

"JACQUES!" Her scream was raw, primal, lost amidst the cacophony of destruction.

Renée stumbled to her feet, her body moving on instinct as she sprinted towards the devastation. Tears mingled with rain, blurring her sight but not her resolve. Her heart thundered in her chest, a rapid drumbeat echoing the terror that gripped her soul.

"Please, no," she whispered, a mantra against despair. "Not Jacques."

The man who'd charmed her with his laughter, whose sadness she'd glimpsed in unguarded moments, couldn't be gone. Not when they had only just begun to weave the threads of their lives together.

Through the haze of her shock, Renée Vanslambrouck realised one immutable truth: nothing would ever be the same again.

Renée's hands were a blur against the rubble, bloodied and unrecognisable as fragments of brick and mortar bit into her skin. Adrenaline surged through her veins, each piece she tore away fuelled by a single, desperate hope: to find Jacques alive.

"JACQUES!" Her voice was hoarse, every shout a testament to their shared dreams and whispered secrets. She ignored the sting of masonry fragments in her open wounds, the chill of the wind as it whipped through her blouse and skirt, the once-pristine fabric now stained with soot and despair. The sirens of emergency vehicles grew louder.

Around her, the emergency crews worked with mechanical precision, their faces set in grim determination as they pulled at the debris. Townspeople, too, came to assist, forming a human chain, passing broken bricks and twisted metal hand to hand, unified in their efforts to rescue those trapped beneath.

A woman's scream – a raw, guttural sound – erupted from somewhere close by, followed by the muffled cries of others entombed within the cinema's remains. Renée's heart seized with each cry; they were the sounds of life, of possibility. She redoubled her efforts, her nails splitting against the hard surfaces.

"Keep back, miss! It's not safe!" A fireman tried to pull her away, but she shook him off with unexpected strength.

"Let go! I have to find him!" Renée spat out the words, her assertive voice betraying no hint of the fear ripping through her core. She turned back to the wreckage, her movements frenzied, her vision tunnelled on saving the man who'd brought laughter back into her life.

"Miss! You're hurt!" A nurse, her face smudged with ash, reached for Renée's hands, enveloping them in a clean cloth. The sudden touch startled Renée, breaking her trance. She looked down, seeing the damage for the first time – deep lacerations crisscrossing her palms, the crimson stark against the white gauze.

"Let me help you," the nurse insisted, guiding Renée to the rear of an ambulance. The reality of her own vulnerability washed over her in an icy wave, but it was the thought of Jacques lying cold and still that made her shiver uncontrollably.

"Please, no ..." The words tumbled from Renée's lips, a fervent prayer to a sky darkened by smoke and sorrow.

"Sit down." The nurse's voice was firm but not unkind as she began cleaning Renée's wounds with practised care. "You've done all you can. They'll find him."

But Renée's eyes, fixed on the ruins, saw only a grave. A tomb for the hundreds who had come to escape into the fantasies of the silver screen, now trapped in a nightmare from which there was no waking.

And Jacques ...

If he was gone, what remained of her world? What was left but the echo of his laughter, the ghost of his touch?

"Please," Renée whispered to the sky, a wordless plea for mercy in a merciless moment. It was a plea to God – for Jacques, for herself, for a future that might never be.

"Rest now," the nurse soothed, wrapping bandages around the worst of the cuts. But rest was a distant dream, a luxury afforded to those untouched by tragedy. For Renée, there would be no peace, not until she knew Jacques' fate — for better or worse.

He had to be alive. He simply had to be.

***

The shrill ring of the telephone pierced through the silence of Renée's small, dimly lit living room — a sharp reminder that life persisted outside her flat. With a trembling hand, she lifted the receiver to her ear, bracing for news she wasn't sure she could bear.

"Renée? It's Tom," came the voice from the other end, each word crackling over the line like distant gunfire. "We've found Jacques."

Time halted, the air in her lungs turning to ice. "Is he ...?"

"Alive. Barely. He's at the Medway Maritime Hospital, but he hasn't come round yet." Tom's voice was a blend of relief and caution, a lifeline thrown across the abyss of Renée's despair.

She dropped the receiver; it dangled by its cord, swinging like a pendulum as she raced out, slamming the door behind her.

***

On the wall of the hospital ward the clock ticked incessantly, marking the seconds slipping by, while Jacques lay motionless on the bed, his body a map of bandages and bruises. Renée perched beside him, her hand enveloping his, clinging to the warmth that assured her he was still with her.

"Come back to me, Jacques," she whispered into the sterile silence, her words a mantra against the hushed footsteps of nurses outside the room. "You must."

Night bled into day, and then into night again, a cycle unending. Renée spoke to the unconscious figure before her – of dances they'd missed, of quiet Ostend parks without the thunder of war, of a future that hung in the balance, tethered to the fragile rise and fall of his chest.

On the sixth day, as dawn crept through the blinds, casting stripes across the white walls, something shifted. Jacques' eyelids fluttered, a subtle protest against the brightening room. Renée leaned in, her breath caught between hope and fear.

"Jacques?" Her voice broke the morning's calm.

His eyes opened – a glimmer of blue in a sea of red and swollen flesh. Recognition flickered in them, weak but undeniable.

"Renée ..." His voice was a rasp, barely audible above the hum of machinery.

Tears spilled down her cheeks, washing away the remnants of terror. He was back. He was alive. And in that moment, the world, with all its chaos and ruin, receded – leaving only the bond between two souls who had been torn apart by war, now reunited in the quiet sanctity of a hospital ward.

Renée's hand hovered over Jacques' as he drifted in and out of sleep, his bandaged head an eerie contrast to the smooth white of the pillow beneath it. His chest rose and fell with a ragged consistency that belied the turmoil churning within his unconscious mind.

Suddenly, Jacques' body jerked, a spasm that sent a jolt through Renée's spine. His lips parted, and from them spilled tormented cries that clawed at the silence.

"Ana ... no!"

The name was a plea, torn from the depths of a haunted dream. Renée's heart clenched; her eyes widened in alarm.

"Kamia ... my love ... Papa is coming."

The words were a gut-wrenching echo of sorrow and longing.

"Who are you calling for?" Renée whispered into the sterile air, the names unfamiliar, their weight heavy with implications she couldn't grasp. Fear knotted in her stomach as she watched Jacques' face contort with anguish. Each cry was a sliver of doubt wedging itself into the trust she'd placed in him. Who were these women? What past clung to him, a shadow she could not see?

Her thoughts raced, a tumultuous storm that mirrored the chaos enveloping Jacques' restless sleep. Her fingers tightened around his, willing him calm, willing him back to her and away from the phantoms that held him captive.

"Miss Vanslambrouck?"

The sudden voice startled Renée, and she turned to find the doctor standing in the doorway, a look of concern etched upon his features. She stood quickly, brushing away the questions that had seeded themselves in her mind.

"Doctor," she acknowledged with a nod, her voice steady despite the tremors of uncertainty that threatened to break through.

"Did you know that Jacques has malaria?" The doctor's question was a simple one, but it struck Renée like a blow. *Malaria?*

"Excuse me?" Her assertiveness faltered, her response tinged with disbelief. "Malaria?"

"Yes," the doctor confirmed, stepping closer. "It's quite likely contributing to his delirium. It's important we know his medical history to provide the best care."

Renée shook her head, confusion and frustration swirling within her. "He never mentioned ... I didn't know."

She glanced back at Jacques, his murmurs now a soft litany in the quiet room. The revelation of his illness was another piece of the puzzle she hadn't known existed – a life he'd lived without her, filled with secrets and shadows that seemed to loom ever larger.

"Thank you, Doctor," Renée managed to say, her voice a hollow shell of her usual confidence. "I ... I'll have to ask him when he's better."

As the doctor left, promising to return with more information, Renée sat back down beside Jacques, her gaze lingering on his pained expression. The seeds of doubt had taken root, sprouting fears she could neither quell nor comprehend. The man she loved was an enigma, shrouded in mysteries that bridged continents and echoed with the names of strangers.

In the sterile confines of the hospital room, Renée felt the distance between them growing, an expanse far greater than the few inches of mattress that separated their hands. And somewhere in the space between certainty and the unknown, her heart ached for answers she feared might shatter her world completely.

The sterile hospital light assaulted Jacques' senses as he clawed back into consciousness. He registered the weight of bandages swathing his head and the dull ache in his ankles before the sight of Renée beside him came into focus. Her face was a mask of concern, but her eyes, usually so full of life, were clouded with something dark and unreadable.

"Renée," Jacques' voice rasped, laden with the relief of seeing her there. But the warmth he expected in return never came.

"Who are Ana and Kamia?" Renée cut through the silence like a blade, her tone sharp and unforgiving. "And how in God's name do you have malaria?"

Jacques felt the room spin, the shadows of his past creeping up behind his eyes. He had hoped to spare her from this history, from the ghosts that haunted his every step. Taking a painful breath, he began his confession, his words stumbling over one another in their haste to emerge.

"Ana was ... she was my love. In the Congo, we ... and Kamia, our daughter." His throat tightened around the truth he had buried deep within him for too long. The air between them grew heavy as he recounted his youth, the vibrant life he'd lived in Africa, and the violence that tore it all away. Jacques didn't stop there ... it all came spilling out of him ... the Gestapo torture in the Miranda camp and how he would never be able to give Renée a family. He owed her the whole truth.

Renée recoiled as if struck, her face pale, her body rigid. "You lied to me," she whispered, the hurt in her voice more piercing than anger. "You kept your past hidden ... and now what? What else have you not told me? And what about our future ... no children, Jacques? Really?"

Jacques reached out to her, seeking forgiveness, seeking the touch that might bridge the chasm that yawned between them. But she retreated from his grasp, her decision etched into the lines of her face.

"I can't do this … it's all too much," she said, and with those words, raced out of the room, out of his life, leaving him alone with an endlessly ticking clock and the mess of secrets finally laid bare.

***

Convalescing in his apartment in Chatham, Jacques' world shrank to the confines of four walls. Daylight seeped through the curtains, indifferent to the man whose soul was being consumed by darkness. Once robust and commanding, Jacques now lay curled on his side, the whispers of his past clawing their way into every waking moment.

He saw Ana's smile flicker in the shadows, heard Kamia's laughter in the silence that suffocated him. The sense of loss was a physical pain, a relentless torment that gripped him tighter with each solitary hour. He had survived war and prison camps, but the absence of Renée's presence was an agony no experience had prepared him for.

Kamia … my gorgeous girl … Papa is coming.

His own voice mocked him from memory, a cruel reminder of promises he couldn't keep, of a future that was slipping through his fingers like grains of sand.

Jacques hadn't realised how much he had come to rely on Renée's strength, her unyielding spirit that had pulled him from the depths once before. But now, her absence left him adrift in a sea of remorse, a tide of helplessness that threatened to drown him.

A photo of them together, smiling at some forgotten joke, lay discarded on the floor. He reached for it, his hands trembling, and allowed himself a single moment of weakness, clinging to the image as though it could somehow restore what had been lost. But the paper felt cold and lifeless in his grip, an unwanted memory of happier times.

"Forgive me," he whispered to the empty room, a plea to ghosts who did not answer. With each laboured breath, Jacques sank deeper into the abyss, a man fractured by war, haunted by love, and betrayed by his own secrets.

The door creaked open, sending a sliver of light slicing through the gloom that had become Jacques' personal purgatory. Two days had passed since Renée had gone, two days that had stretched and contorted into an interminable expanse of time in which he wrestled with his own demons.

Jacques didn't turn to look at the intruder; his gaze remained fixated on the grainy texture of the floorboards, as if they concealed some answer to the riddle of his suffering. He felt the presence enter, a shift in the air, a disturbance in the oppressive atmosphere of the room.

"Renée?" His voice was a hoarse whisper, an echo of the man who once charmed crowds and defied oppressors.

"Look at me, Jacques."

It was her voice, unmistakably laced with the assertiveness that could cut through his despair. He lifted his head slowly, almost fearing the sight of her – afraid that she was nothing more than a figment of his fractured mind.

But there she stood, her features etched with determination, glasses glinting in the muted light, pearls resting against her blouse – a vision of 1940s resilience. In her hands, she clutched a piece of paper like a lifeline.

"I've got something for you," Renée said, her voice softer now but still unwavering. "An address ... in Brussels ... for the orphanage records in the Belgian Foreign Office."

Jacques' heart lurched. The possibility of rekindling the search for Kamia sparked like a flame in the cold hearth of his soul. Cautiously, he rose to his feet, his body protesting each movement with memories of injuries both old and new.

"Renée, I ..." he began, but she silenced him with a raised hand.

"It's OK, Jacques." She strode forward and pressed the paper into his palm, folding her fingers around his hands. "I don't know what we'll find, or if we'll find anything at all. But if there's even a chance, we have to take it. Together."

Her words pierced through the fog that clouded his thoughts. A wave of relief flooded his body, tears streaming down his scarred cheeks. This was hope, a rare and precious commodity he thought he had lost.

"Renée, why?" He searched her face, looking for the traces of the anger he expected, the resentment he deserved.

"Because I realised that I love you. No matter what you've been through in the past, I still love you now, in the present. And if you'll have me ... every part of me is saying I can't live without you, Jacques Dumont," she confessed, her usual bravado giving way to vulnerability. "We will find her, Jacques. We'll bring her home ... and we'll make a family."

Jacques' eyes continued to glisten with tears, a tempest of emotions threatening to flood. Renée reached out, her touch grounding him, anchoring him back to the present.

"Let's start again," she urged. "You and me."

"Thank you," he murmured, cradling her hand against his chest where his heart beat for her, renewed by the promise of redemption.

She offered him a smile, genuine and bright, a beacon in the storm that had been his existence. It was all the reply he needed.

In that moment, Jacques understood that Renée was more than a partner; she was his North Star in the darkness, the joy amidst haunting memories. And as they embraced, the shadows that had once seemed indelible began to recede, replaced by the comfort of a shared future.

Chapter 10:
1948 (Jacques, aged 33)

The bracing North Sea breeze whipped around Jacques as he stepped out onto the balcony of their newly acquired apartment overlooking Ostend. He leaned on the railing, casting his gaze over the Mercator yacht harbour where warships had once dominated the skyline. Now, pleasure boats bobbed in their berths, and the air carried the sound of reconstruction, not conflict. Most of the shops, including his old bakery, had been decimated as the Allied Forces pushed back tyranny. New buildings were being hurriedly constructed all over the town.

"Quite a view, isn't it?" Renée's voice broke through his reverie, her hand warm on his shoulder. They shared a moment, silent acknowledgment of the city rising from its own ashes.

"Buildings seem to grow back bigger and stronger; if only humans could do the same," Jacques murmured, his eyes reflecting both the sky and the water below.

"Good luck for the job interview, my love," Renée chirped with characteristic assertiveness. Jacques raised a smile.

"Ah, if they only knew that behind every great man is an even greater woman."

Wrapping her up in a bear hug, she saw admiration for her etched on his face.

Renée adjusted his tie, a pop of colour against his crisp white shirt. "Just be yourself. Charm them in every language you know."

"*Nakupenda sana*," he whispered, kissing Renée's forehead, then slipped from her grasp like a ship from its mooring, off to navigate the choppy waters of the Royal Flandrian Yacht Club's hiring process.

The club itself had been rebuilt quickly from the rubble of war, and its spirit returned as quickly as the pleasure cruisers and sailing boats. As Jacques entered the building, the soles of his polished brogues clicked authoritatively on the polished floors, echoing off the walls. The panel of interviewers awaited him in a room with wide windows that overlooked the harbour, a strategic reminder of what was at stake.

"Mr Dumont," greeted the commodore, a man with a weathered face like an old mariner's map. "We've heard much about your exploits."

"Thank you," Jacques replied, maintaining direct eye contact, his posture a blend of military precision and relaxed confidence.

"Your résumé speaks of multilingual proficiency," another member noted, tapping on the papers before him.

"Indeed," Jacques confirmed, ready to switch between languages at a moment's notice, his words smooth and articulate.

"I believe communication is the keel of understanding in any port."

"Show us," challenged the third man, scepticism threaded through his tone.

Without missing a beat, Jacques transitioned from Dutch to French, Portuguese to German, Spanish to Swahili, and back to English, each sentence flowing seamlessly into the next. The panel members exchanged glances, some nodding appreciatively at his display.

"Very impressive," the chairman conceded. "And your maritime experience?"

"Three years in the navy," Jacques recounted, the memories glancing momentarily across his charismatic expression. "Navigating both men and vessels through turbulent times."

They probed further, asking intricate questions about sailing, tides and harbour management. Each query Jacques fielded with the deftness of a seasoned sailor catching the wind, his responses laced with an undercurrent of passion for the sea and the peace it now represented.

As the interview drew to a close, the panel members looked amongst themselves. Jacques couldn't read their expressions.

"Thank you, Mr Dumont," the chairman finally said. "You'll be hearing from us."

Jacques nodded, his heart a vessel caught in the doldrums awaiting the breeze of their decision. He left the room, the sense of being evaluated lingering like the chill of the sea breeze outside.

Back at the apartment, Renée watched from the balcony as Jacques returned. She could tell nothing from his walk, nothing from the set of his shoulders. With swift steps, he ascended to their new home overlooking Ostend, where their future in this resurrected city hung in balance, as delicate and as promising as the horizon at dawn.

The sun had begun its descent, casting a golden hue over the room where Jacques and Renée sat at an old oak table strewn with papers. The rhythmic scratch of their pens against the parchment emphasised their anxieties. Each letter they penned to the Belgian Foreign Office and the Ministry of Social Welfare was a shot in the dark, a plea for a trace of Kamia.

"Perhaps she's no longer called 'Kamia'," Jacques murmured, his voice barely lifting from the paper. His hand was steady, but the lines he wrote bore the weight of his desperation.

"Let's just keep trying," Renée insisted, her glasses reflecting the resolve in her eyes. "Every letter is a step closer."

Days turned into weeks, and each envelope returned carried the same dismissive message: "We cannot help you." The words echoed through the empty spaces of their home, resonating with the hollowness that had settled in their chests.

Undeterred, their quest took them to the heart of bureaucracy. The drive to Brussels was long and silent, anticipation gnawing at their insides like a relentless tide against the cliffs. They arrived under the shadow of imposing government buildings, monoliths of power that could either reunite or forever separate them from her.

They waited, hours stretching thin their patience, in a stuffy office that reeked of dust and indifference. When finally ushered into the presence of the administrative supervisor, hope flickered briefly before being snuffed out by his disdainful glance.

"Jacques Dumont," the man said, his voice utterly ambivalent. "You come seeking what? A *métis* child lost in the chaos of a war-torn world? Have you any idea how many of those children are now in the system? It's like—"

"I know," interrupted Jacques, "a needle in a haystack," he finished. "And she's not a lost child … her name is Kamia," Jacques corrected him, fighting to keep his tone level. "She's my daughter, taken from us by your government. Surely there must be records … something."

"Mr Dumont," the supervisor cut him off with a wave of his hand as if swatting away an irksome fly. "Your story is not unique. Many have lost loved ones, and many have suffered. We simply do not have the resources to track every displaced person. Herr Hitler did not care for the blacks, you see – so many of them simply 'vanished'."

Renée rose to her feet beside Jacques, her assertiveness a vibrant flame. "But you must understand—"

"Madame," the supervisor interjected, "I understand more than you think. But understanding does not equate to miracles. I'm sorry. There's nothing we can do."

Their pleas fell on deaf ears, and they were summarily dismissed, left to navigate the labyrinth of corridors back to the daylight. The cool air outside did little to ease the stifling sense of defeat.

As they drove back to Ostend, the silence between Jacques and Renée was louder than any argument. It was the sound of unyielding red tape, of doors slammed shut, of a daughter who at best was lost in a system that didn't care, and at worst was dead at the hands of the Nazis.

The apartment was quiet, too quiet – as if the walls themselves were holding their breath, waiting for a sign that would never come. Jacques stood by the window, his gaze fixed on the murky waters of the harbour where the Mercator yacht held fast against its moorings, with tourists teeming over it like ants. The setting sun cast long shadows over the water, a stark contrast to the bright future he had once envisioned.

In his hand, he clutched the latest letter from the Ministry, the words "We have no records matching the name Kamia Dumont" glaring up at him like an accusation. Each syllable pounded in his head, a relentless echo of the finality that seemed to seep into his very bones. He crumpled the paper in his fist, the gesture void of the anger that had once fuelled him. Now, there was nothing left but an emptiness that gnawed at his insides.

Renée moved about the apartment with a mechanical efficiency. There were no words, nothing she could say that would help ease the heartache. She avoided meeting his eyes, perhaps unable or unwilling to confront the shared despair that hung between them.

"Renée." Jacques' voice broke the silence, barely more than a whisper, raw and edged with the pain of hopelessness.

She turned to him, her own eyes pools of unshed tears. No words passed between them; none were needed. In her face, he saw the reflection of his own defeat.

He retreated from the window, his movements heavy, lethargic. Not so much as a photograph to remember her by.

Jacques sank into a chair, the wood creaking under the weight of his despondence.

He had failed to protect his daughter as a baby.

Now he was failing her all over again.

Just like he failed her mother.

And there it was again … the most self-sabotaging emotion of them all. Shame felled Jacques harder than any Gestapo beating.

His journey had been for nothing. So many miles. So many times he cheated death through sheer determination to reach her. So many dreams of his little baby girl, with perfect skin, her mother's tight curls and his blue eyes. He had failed her, and the shame cut him through.

As darkness fell, enveloping the room in its sombre embrace, Jacques' mind drifted out to sea, lost amidst the waves of uncertainty. He thought of Kamia, the wrinkle of her nose when she laughed, the sound of her voice calling out "Papa" – her very first word.

"Where are you, Kamia?" he murmured to the empty room, to the night, to a world that had turned its back on a little girl caught in its historical crossfire. There was no answer, only the distant sound of the North Sea, indifferent and relentless, carrying away the last vestiges of a father's hope on the outgoing tide.

Chapter 11:
1968 (Jacques, aged 53)

Jacques Dumont's leathery hands, although creaking with a twinge of arthritis, still danced with seasoned agility over the coarse ropes, securing another yacht to the weathered pontoons with practised knots. His eyes, still sharp despite the passing years, flickered across the harbour's mosaic of flags, a silent testament to the sailors' multicultural origins. As he collected the mooring fees, his lips parted to offer thanks in the native tongue of each seafarer, a linguistic performance that never ceased to delight the visitors.

"*Merci, mon ami.*" He smiled warmly at a French skipper, switching seamlessly to Dutch for the next: "*Dank u wel.*" A murmur of impressed chuckles spread through the small crowd gathered at the yacht club café. They watched as this ageing man, whose blond hair had surrendered to the silver of time, moved with a nimble grace that belied his years.

The sun had begun to set, casting long shadows from the quayside across the marina, when the discordant strains of loud music and boisterous laughter shattered the tranquil evening air. Jacques, sensing the growing irritation among the other sailors, approached the cause of the commotion – an expensive 50-foot-long yacht, *The Siren*. *How apt*, thought Jacques, as the affluent owners partied raucously without concern for peace or propriety.

"*Excusez-moi, mesdames et messieurs*," Jacques called out, his voice firm yet courteous as he boarded the vessel uninvited but undeterred. The revellers, adorned in Rolex watches and diamond earrings that sparkled under the festoon lights, turned their pampered faces towards him.

"Could we perhaps keep the celebration to a more ... moderate level?" Jacques suggested, offering a conciliatory smile that reached the lines around his eyes, the same eyes that had once searched through darkness for signs of enemy movement, now searching for a glimmer of understanding.

"Who is this?" sneered a man with a silk cravat, his words slurred by intoxication. "The harbour master or the entertainment?"

The crowd erupted into laughter, their champagne flutes clinking in mockery. A woman in a dress that sparkled like the sea under moonlight leaned forward, her red lips parting in disdain.

"Perhaps he thinks he's one of us," she cooed, laughter lilting in her voice. "A simple rope monkey who takes our money and now our orders – another G&T for me, old man." More cackling ensued.

Stung by the insult, Jacques felt the familiar burn of indignity simmer beneath his weathered skin. But he stood his ground, his back straight as a mast, though no one here knew of the Croix de Guerre medals that once adorned his chest or the sacrifices that earned them. He had confronted far graver threats than silver spoons and snide remarks, and besides, no words could hurt any deeper than the torment of shame he had heaped upon himself.

"Please," he persisted, the word carrying the weight of unspoken battles, "for the comfort of your fellow sailors."

But the yacht's snobbish owner simply waved him away with an air of entitled superiority. With no other recourse, Jacques offered a polite nod and retreated to his hut, the cacophony of the party trailing behind him like the jeers of ghosts from a past life.

There, under the stars that once guided him across Europe, Jacques tasted disrespect once more. He was just a harbour master after all, reduced to a mere shadow in the eyes of those who knew nothing of honour or sacrifice. And the man who once shone with the bravado of resistance against oppression finally submitted to defeat.

Without Kamia, he was beaten. She had been his compass, his why, his reason to stay alive.

Jacques questioned whether staying alive was worth it any more. It was only Renée that kept him here.

***

Winter was on its way and the yacht club pontoons emptied of visitors. Jacques' muscles ached with the bitter North Sea chill as he scraped the pungent seaweed and tenacious barnacles from the slick pillars that held the pontoons in place, his movements rhythmic and hollow against the backdrop of a leaden sky. The waves lapped up through the wooden slats at his boots, insidious in their icy caress, creeping through the seams to numb his skin. His breaths emerged in ragged plumes, each one dissipating into the cold, uncaring air.

"Has it come to this?" he murmured to himself, a hollow whisper lost amidst the mournful cries of the gulls overhead. Once a man who commanded respect, reduced now to wrestling with the unforgiving sea for sustenance. Each pull of the dark vegetation felt as if he was peeling away pieces of his once indomitable spirit.

The job done, Jacques trudged towards his sanctuary, the cramped harbour master's hut — a refuge that did little to keep out the onslaught of winter's melancholy. Inside, the electric heater offered a feeble protest against the pervasive chill, its warmth a mere echo of the potbelly stove that had once been a lifeline of survival in the Miranda camp.

He sank into the threadbare office chair, his body folding into itself like a weathered map worn by too many hands. Memories of the Congo flickered in the heat's weak glow, taunting him with their ghostly presence. The past clung to him, an unshakeable shadow that darkened even the most mundane tasks of his current existence.

The sudden tap on the glass shattered his depression, a sharp punctuation in the silence. Jacques' gaze snapped to the window, where a pair of blue eyes — mirroring his own yet framed by a frizz of African hair — gazed back at him.

Time stopped.

There was something familiar about this young woman's smile, warm and tentative amidst the trails of tears – a stark contrast to the cold grey world outside.

Jacques lurched to his feet, joints protesting, as he moved towards her. The door swung open with a creak.

They embraced each other instinctively.

Kamia had come for him.

And her smile filled the sparse confines of the little hut like sunlight streaming through storm clouds.

Jacques held her tightly, sobbing uncontrollably into her coat.

"I missed you, Papa."

He would never let go.

Never.

Kamia's Story

1940

The truck's engine growled a deep, throaty protest as Sofia De Vries manoeuvred it through the blackened streets of Brussels, nearing their destination. The beams of its headlights pierced the pre-dawn darkness, each jolt and swerve a battle against time. Behind her, the groans and whispered prayers of the hospital patients she ferried mingled with the staccato rhythm of shelling in the distance. The fate of the city of Leuven hung on a precipice, and with each passing moment, the noose of the Third Reich drew tighter. Evacuation had been their only option.

"Almost there," Sofia murmured to herself, the grip on the steering wheel betraying none of her inner turmoil. Her slender but strong physique leaned into each turn, her shoulder-length red hair, normally neatly tied back, now wild and untamed. *This was not what I got into nursing for,* she mused.

As the hospital, Clinique Saint-Jean, loomed into view along the Boulevard du Jardin Botanique, a sanctuary of stone amidst chaos, Sofia exhaled a sigh that carried the weight of countless lives. She swung the truck into the main emergency entrance, and porters rushed out to assist its precious cargo. Noticing Sofia's fraught dishevelled appearance, another nurse, clad in the crisp white uniform of Saint-Jean, was at her side.

"Mademoiselle De Vries," the nurse said, her voice firm yet tinged with warmth. "We've got it from here. Please, let us take care of you now."

Sofia nodded, her green eyes scanning the organised frenzy as staff unloaded patients, their movements precise despite the urgency. She allowed herself to be led away, her senses still attuned to the sounds of suffering that she had become all too familiar with.

"Here, drink this." A cup of hot, black coffee was pressed into her hands, the aroma cutting through the fog of exhaustion.

"Thank you," Sofia replied, her heightened state of alert now softening with gratitude. As she sipped, she watched the nurses working; a symphony of efficiency and empathy. It was here among these kindred spirits that she would find her new place in this war-torn world. The ancient establishment of Leuven University Hospital, the place Sofia had trained like thousands of clinicians centuries before her, would be in ruins by noon.

"Come," the nurse urged after a moment. "Let me show you where you'll be staying."

The nursing accommodation block was a short walk from the main hospital building, its walls steady and unassuming. Inside, corridors held the echo of footsteps long past, leading them to an apartment marked with a freshly painted number.

"Your new home," the nurse announced, pushing open the door.

The room beyond was modest, a spartan setup with a few beds and personal lockers. Yet, there was comfort in its simplicity, a promise of camaraderie and shared purpose. Three new room-mates turned to greet Sofia, their faces worn with lines of fatigue and resolve.

"Everyone, this is Sofia DeVries," the nurse introduced. "She's been evacuating patients from Leuven."

"Welcome," one of them said, stepping forward with an outstretched hand. "I'm Anne-Marie, this is Clara, and that's Josette. We stick together here. Would you like to borrow some of our clothes and toiletries until you get up on your feet?"

"Thank you, that's kind," Sofia replied, meeting each gaze with her own. "I'm ready to do my part."

Their nods were all the assurance she needed. In the heart of an occupied city, amidst the shadows of uncertainty, Sofia De Vries found her new front-line.

The wail of sirens cut through the dusk as Nurse De Vries adjusted the taut bandage around a soldier's thigh, her fingers working deftly even as the ground shuddered with distant explosions. Clinique Saint-Jean had become a crucible of life and death, echoing with the cacophony of war – groans of pain, shouts for assistance, and the relentless march of boots.

"Pressure here, don't let go," Sofia instructed a volunteer, placing his hands over the wound. Her green eyes, sharp and focused, scanned the makeshift triage area for the next critical case. Every bed was occupied; every surface became an examination table.

She moved with a certainty honed by intensive experience – every day the learning curve grew steeper; all the while her strength and clear thinking under pressure was tested to breaking point. The capitulation of Brussels had thrust her into a world where her desire to care morally collided with the harsh realities of occupation. Sofia found herself having to treat enemy soldiers. General von Falkenhausen's regime cast a shadow over the city, oppressing its people with fear and control, yet within these walls, she found ways to defy that darkness.

1944

Months turned into years, and the shortages grew dire. "We need more O negative!" she called out, her voice cutting through the clamour. The supply room echoed back empty. Blood was a currency they couldn't afford to waste, and every drop counted in this desperate economy.

"Use mine," she offered without hesitation, rolling up her sleeve. There was no time for self-preservation when lives hung in the balance.

"Another blast victim coming through!" The warning cry preceded the hurried arrival of stretcher-bearers carrying a man peppered with shrapnel, his face a mask of shock and blood.

"Clear a space!" demanded Sofia, assertive and undaunted as she guided them through the labyrinth of suffering. She assessed the wounds with clinical precision, the red hair that had been neatly presentable at the start of her shift now ragged and wild, her attire practical – trousers and blouse beneath a nurse's apron, smeared with the evidence of tireless medical labour.

"Clamp! Quick!" She barked orders, and the hospital team responded as one – a united front against the tide of casualties that flowed through their doors. They had become a family forged in adversity, each member dependent on the others, each victory shared, each loss mourned together.

"Stay with me," Sofia urged her patient, her calm demeanour a lifeline in the storm. As she worked to remove shards of metal from flesh, her mind raced with the logistics of rationing their dwindling resources. Medicines were as scarce as hope, bandages were rewashed and reused, and food was a luxury many could not afford.

Yet, amidst it all, Sofia's protective nature never wavered. Each person under her watch felt the strength of her commitment, the depth of her compassion. She fought for them with every stitch and every soothing word, standing her ground against the encroaching despair.

As night fell and the sirens faded, leaving only the whispers of the wounded and the exhausted sighs of the staff, Sofia remained vigilant. She knew too well that the dawn would bring new challenges, new faces of Brussels' citizens marred by war. But she also knew that as long as she drew breath, she would care deeply for every one of those held captive. It amazed Sofia how a smile and some gentle optimism could keep patients going.

And, every so often, Sofia's optimism was renewed. She would delight in receiving infrequent letters from her big brother, Wout. As the occupation progressed, Sofia's fingers began to tremble slightly as she unfolded each letter from Wout, increasingly worried about what its contents would reveal. Her eyes scanned over his precise handwriting that always seemed too formal for such personal correspondence, like someone other than his sister would be reading it. Despite the distance and the war-hardened exterior he presented to the world, his words brought comfort to Sofia amidst the relentless toll of her nursing duties.

"My dearest Sofia," the latest missive began, "I trust this finds you in good health. Ostend offers me a different vantage point on this senseless conflict. How I long for the days when my greatest concern was the administrative challenges of colonial affairs, rather than the scarcity of freedom ..."

She smiled faintly at the memory of Wout's stories about the Congo, his ambitions so vivid against the backdrop of their childhood memories. He would recount tales of vast lush landscapes and intricate politics, his voice taking on an animated edge she rarely heard. Sofia clung to those moments, reminders of the brother who once shielded her from schoolyard bullies and taught her to stand up for the people she cared about.

Tucking the letter into her pocket, Sofia stepped out into the grey Brussels morning, determined to find some vegetables for the hospital kitchen. The streets bustled with hushed activity; wary eyes flitted about, each exchange a silent rebellion against the occupation's stranglehold.

As she turned down a narrow alleyway shortcut, a firm hand yanked her aside, pulling Sofia into the shadows. Her heart leapt for an instant, before recognising, to her utter delight, the intense grey eyes of her brother.

"Wout! What are you—" she began, her voice a whispered shriek.

"Quiet, Sofia," he cut in, urgency etched into every line of his face. "I don't have much time. Things are in motion – big things. We're going to hit them where it hurts."

A chill ran down Sofia's spine. She had heard rumours of the resistance, of daring plots unfolding in secret, but to hear Wout speak of them made the danger achingly real.

"Please, be careful brother," she implored, her protective instincts surging. "You mustn't get caught."

Wout's smile was grim, a shadow of his usual bravado. "If anything happens to me, Laurens van Huysen will handle my affairs. Promise me you'll stay safe, Fifi."

His use of her childhood nickname registered the gravity of the situation, and she fought back tears. "I promise. And you …"

In that timeless moment, as they embraced each other tightly, everything between them was love. Eventually, Wout kissed her tenderly on the cheek.

Sofia's goodbyes were lost as the brother she adored melted into the maze of alleys, leaving her sickened for his fate. She took a deep breath for composure, uttered a prayer towards the sky for God's mercy, and went about her errands.

***

In the dim glow of a single bulb, Sofia De Vries' shadow danced against the stone walls as she administered some aspirin to a small, shivering boy hidden in the makeshift dormitory beneath Clinique Saint-Jean. The basement sanctuary had become a clandestine refuge for the children nobody was meant to find. Their gaunt faces, smiles weak with the uncertainty of war, often haunted Sofia's dreams, but she remained steadfast – always compassionate amidst chaos. None of them would see their parents again. She was their mother right now.

"Shh, it will be over soon," she whispered, her voice a soothing balm in the cold basement air.

"Will they come for us?" The child's voice cracked, his blue eyes wide and searching in the half-light.

Sofia gently brushed his hair back from his forehead. "Not while I'm here," she promised, though her heart raced at the thought of being discovered. Every day was a delicate balance between life and the lurking spectre of a raid by the SS.

1945

Months bled into one another, blurring in an endless cycle of whispered lullabies and silent prayers until one autumn morning when the distant rumble of liberation thundered through Brussels like the first rains after a long drought.

"*Allemaal naar buiten!*" the call echoed down the hallways, and Sofia emerged, squinting against the bright sunlight that bathed the liberated city. Cheers and cries of joy filled the streets, a cacophony of relief that swelled in her chest. She hugged her colleagues, their tired faces breaking into wide, incredulous smiles. They had survived; they had persevered.

"*Vrijheid*! Freedom!" The words were a sweet melody, and Sofia joined in the chorus, her laughter mingling with the tears that streamed freely down her face. For a moment, the weight of the world lifted, replaced by the heady sensation of hope.

But as the celebrations waned and life began to stitch itself back together, a telegram arrived like a cold hand on Sofia's shoulder.

"Nurse De Vries," Doctor Ricard called out, stepping through the door of the nurses' quarters, his face grave as he extended the slip of paper.

Sofia's hands trembled as she unfolded the message, her eyes scanning the words that would cleave her world in two:

'Your brother Wout captured and executed alongside comrades last year. Bravery in the face of the enemy till the end. Deepest condolences. – Marcel.'

The room spun, and she gripped the edge of a table for support. Tears blurred her vision as she re-read the lines, hoping for some mistake, some reprieve from this cruel twist. But the truth bore into her like a bullet, hollowing out her elation and leaving only despair.

Wout – her protector, her confidant, the brother who had defended her honour in schoolyard scuffles and consoled her through childhood nightmares – was gone. His final act, a daring assault on the very heart of the enemy, snuffed out by betrayal and the cold machinery of war.

"*Godverdomme*," she cursed under her breath, a rare slip of anger that betrayed the turmoil within. She would mourn, yes, but she would also remember him as he lived: resolute, brave, fighting for a cause he believed in. In the quiet hush of the hospital, surrounded by those she had shielded from the storm, Sofia vowed to carry on, for him.

Peaceful months turned into peaceful years.

1946

Dust motes danced in the air, catching on the light breeze that did little to alleviate the heat. Lina's laughter trilled from the henhouse, a soothing balm to the raw edges of Sofia's grief.

"Careful with those!" Lina called out, her voice brimming with an affection that had become Sofia's lifeline in the wake of Wout's death.

Sofia set the sack down beside the trough and wiped her brow, her gaze drifting beyond the wooden fences to the rows of crops they'd planted together. This land was both an escape and a remembrance; each seed sown was a testament to their love and to the brother who had once been her world. She could almost see Wout among the stalks of corn, his sharp features softened by the golden hue of twilight, but it was just a trick of memory and longing.

"Every day gets a little easier," Sofia murmured, though she suspected the ache might linger for a lifetime. The strength she wielded so confidently as a nurse seemed to falter when faced with this personal loss.

"Hey, gorgeous." Lina beckoned, her arms open and inviting.

Sofia went willingly, seeking refuge in the embrace that promised solace. They shared a kiss and stood amidst their sanctuary, two women bound by love and the shared dream of peace. Here, amidst the tilled earth and the quiet hum of life, they were simply Sofia and Lina, unmarked by the war that had raged around them.

But even as they carved out this space for themselves, the past refused to remain buried. A letter arrived, its seal stark against the worn wood of their mailbox. It was from Laurens van Huysen, the family solicitor. Sofia's heart clenched, her fingers trembling as she turned the envelope over in her hands. Wout's last will and testament. What final message did he leave behind? Could there possibly be any closure in the sterile words of a legal document?

***

"Will you go?" Lina asked, her eyes searching Sofia's face for signs.

"I must," Sofia replied, stoically. "For him. For whatever piece of him still lingers in this world."

Washed and changed out of dirty farm clothes, with a farewell hug from her soulmate, Sofia De Vries ventured into the city. Brussels had come alive again after the oppression of occupation, yet memories lingered in the alleys and corners. Sofia navigated the streets trying to cling to the joyfulness of liberation.

The solicitor's office was a mausoleum of mahogany and leather, hushed whispers echoing off the walls. Solicitor Laurens van Huysen greeted her with a solemn nod, ushering her into the inner sanctum where Wout's last wishes awaited.

"Ms De Vries," he intoned, the formal address a sharp contrast to the intimacy of her grief. "Thank you for coming. I understand that you are Mr De Vries' only surviving relative, is that correct?"

"Yes," Sofia replied, her voice steady for now. Curious, she braced herself for the revelations to come, for the final chapter in Wout's enigmatic life to unfurl before her.

Laurens van Huysen, a man not given to dramatics, placed a package before Sofia with an unusual gentleness. The air in the room felt dense, as if it held the weight of untold stories – tales that could shift the very axis upon which her world turned. Sofia's fingers brushed against the brown paper wrapping, betraying her calm façade.

"Your brother was ... meticulous in his final arrangements," van Huysen said, his voice low and measured. "Please, take your time with these."

Sofia nodded, her throat too tight to form words. She carefully unwrapped the package, revealing a stack of documents bound by a frayed string, aged photographs, and a letter penned in Wout's unmistakable script.

The first photograph she saw was of a young Congolese girl, caught between two worlds in her gaze – the dark depth of her Congolese roots and the clear blue of her Belgian heritage. Sofia inhaled sharply, feeling an inexplicable pull towards a child she had never met. Her hands moved to the records, each document a breadcrumb leading back to a life interrupted by war.

Wout's letter lay beneath them, its edges worn from the journey. Sofia unfolded it with reverence, the ink stark against the yellowed paper:

"My darling sister, if you are reading this you must know that I am with God, the war is over, and I am in no pain. It has been my honour and privilege to be your brother in this life, and after father died in the Great War, I felt it my duty to do my best to take care of you. In my passing, I only ask one thing of you, my dear sister. Please use these documents and funds to find and take into your heart the daughter of one of the bravest men I knew. His name was Jacques Dumont. A more loving father I never did meet. I know not if he is alive after this godforsaken war, or whether he may come looking for her one day, but I do know that I made a promise that I would find her, and I have failed. If you can, please keep her safe and give her the life and love that every child deserves. I know she will be safe in your loving care. Your brother, for eternity, Wout."

His words, a confession and a plea from beyond, clutched at her heart, inducing tears from her eyes. Through blurred vision, she felt his love, duty and a promise unfulfilled – a charge now passed to her.

"Are you alright, Ms De Vries?" Laurens van Huysen's concern broke into her consciousness.

"Thank you, Mr van Huysen," Sofia managed to say, her voice steadier than she felt. "I know what must be done."

She left the office with the package cradled like a newborn against her chest, the cityscape a blur as she navigated the streets back to the farm. The countryside embraced her return, its tranquility a familiar relief for the whirring of her mind.

"Tell me everything," Lina urged as Sofia walked through the door.

"Her name is Kamia," Sofia began, her resolve hardening with each word spoken. She laid out Wout's last wishes, spread the documents on the kitchen table like a detective piecing together clues.

Lina listened, her hand finding Sofia's, their fingers intertwining in shared understanding. They sat together, surrounded by the quiet strength of their farm, the decision forming like a tiny spark in kindling.

"Let's find her, Sofia," Lina said after a while, conviction lighting her features. "We'll find Kamia, and bring her home."

A determined nod was Sofia's answer. They would trace the girl's path, follow the clues Wout left behind, and build a future for Kamia – one filled with the warmth and security of family that this girl deserved. In doing so, they would honour her beloved brother's final wish, healing the wounds of the past with the hope of a future.

The two women began in earnest, contacting each of the dozen or so orphanages in the Brussels district. It quickly became apparent that these institutions were overwhelmed and understaffed, inundated with a tsunami of queries from stricken relatives trying frantically to piece their families back together following the vile separation of war.

They spent days making phone call after phone call ... following up with administrators who had long since filed their query in the waste-paper basket. They became adept at deploying all of the influencing tricks under the sun to encourage action ... the helpless aunt, the angry mother, the lost sister ... and with little progress, despondency began to creep into their actions and words.

At the end of each day, Lina and Sofia would stare at the photo of Wout on their sideboard and regain some motivation to keep going.

Despairing with the lack of success and considering their next option as the farm truck rumbled towards the city market loaded with their produce, Lina decided to visit one of the orphanages in-person, after packing up the stall that afternoon.

The exhausted receptionist at Chez Maman Mimi responded very well to the punnet of cherries that Lina offered as a gesture of empathy and gratitude, and reciprocated with a quick look through the files for a "Kamia Dumont" before departing for the night. Although there was no *métis* by that name in their care, Lina glowed with the satisfaction of discovering a more productive way in. Sofia gave a squeal of excitement later that night, as Lina outlined the new plan to locate her.

They would take Wout's package of information, along with bountiful gifts to "oil the wheels", to every single orphanage in a 20 kilometre radius of Brussels. On rare occasions, a worried expression or pretending to cry would be enough to pity the receptionists and administrators into action … but most of the time pure obstinance worked best – a sheer dogged refusal to leave until the files had been checked.

1948

The wheels of their bicycles churned the dirt road to dust as the women pedalled with determined urgency towards the tram stop. The late afternoon sun cast shadows through the trees, lining the route into the Anderlecht suburbs of the city. Eight months of searching had led them here – to the unkempt grounds of Maison des Hirondelles. It was the very last orphanage on their list, and both women exchanged a doubtful glance as they rang the doorbell.

An elderly gentleman with kind eyes slowly opened the door. The sound of children laughing and shouting emanated from the hallway inside, enveloping the two women on the doorstep, who couldn't help but smile at the raucousness.

Sofia began by explaining that they were searching for a teenager by the name of Kamia Dumont, giving her description and showing some aged photos.

A contemplative look crossed the man's face as he repeated her name. "Kamia … Kamia … hmm, let me think." He was old but something about him conveyed deep wisdom and experience.

"Come in and wait whilst I take a quick look in the files … and then I must return to orchestrating supper."

Sofia and Lina were kept well entertained by two grubby toddlers who immediately approached the women and held their arms aloft as if to request a cuddle. Sofia and Lina obliged, building up enough trust over five minutes to culminate in the blowing of raspberries and much tickling.

"May I see the photograph you showed me again?" he asked.

"Hmm … yes … you see we have a teenage girl here, matching your description, but her name is Kamina Mbala. Kamina arrived from a convent in the Congo in January 1946."

"Mbala?" repeated Sofia excitedly. "The file we have states Ana Mbala as her mother. Do you think her Belgian surname could have been switched?"

"Well, mademoiselles … you'll have to make an official appointment with Mr Directeur here at Hirondelles for any further information, but yes, I've heard of *métis* orphans who've had all traces of their Belgian heritage stripped, replaced by Congolese names – those colonial tyrants couldn't bear to think of them as half-white."

Clearly elated with their discovery, Sofia and Lina hugged the kind gentleman appreciatively, bid fond farewells to the toddlers (who were most upset to be led away from the funny ladies for supper) and made the long journey home, chattering about possibilities all the way.

The following week, both women nervously pressed their hairstyles into place and removed invisible threads from their Sunday best as Lina stretched out to press the doorbell of Home des Hirondelles for a second time.

"We have an appointment with Mr Joubert, the director," Lina announced to the receptionist. "It's about Kamina Mbala."

Joubert worked diligently through their story, painstakingly piecing together details, information, photographs, family connections and proof. After two hours they were all in agreement. Right down to the beads in her hair and those piercing eyes Kamia was Kamina.

Kamia was unsure of them at first, these smiling mzungu women, and although she would never show it, Kamia warmed to them from the start. Each weekly visit deepened their connection, each story shared about Kamia's parents, Jacques and Ana, a thread weaving them into an intricate tapestry of familiarity and trust. Their stories gave her a sense of place in the world. Kamia was 15 now, and of an age when provocative questions and finding one's place felt important.

And then the day came when they would ask for the final piece – Kamia's future entwined with theirs.

"Ready?" Lina smiled, grabbing Sofia's hands and bouncing with nervous energy.

Sofia excitedly returned the squeeze, composed herself, and stepped forward, crossing the threshold between the world they knew and the one they dared to build. The matron, a stern woman with sharp features, awaited them, her gaze wary of the white women who seemed oddly smitten by this *mulâtresse*.

"Mademoiselle Sofia, Mademoiselle Lina," she greeted, a small nod hiding her better judgement.

"We've come for Kamina," Sofia stated, her words clear and unwavering.

The matron regarded them for a moment before calling for the girl. Kamia emerged, her light brown skin glowing against the dim backdrop of the orphanage, blue eyes shifting with curiosity.

In a side room, Sofia began. "Kamia," every syllable imbued with kindness, "we … Lina and I … well … we wondered if you'd like to come to the farm … to live with us … and maybe make a family together."

Lina continued. "You see … we've grown very fond of you, Kamia, and wondered, if … well … we promise to take care of you … make a stable home together … and love you …"

Kamia's gaze shifted between Sofia and Lina, a swirl of emotion playing across her face. Then, with a courage that mirrored the women before her, she nodded in that nonchalant teenage way that belies the joy inside. A simple gesture, with a quarter-smile, that meant the world to all three of them.

"*Oui, ça marche*," she confirmed.

With paperwork signed and farewells exchanged, they departed Maison des Hirondelles with Kamia's worldly possessions packed into a battered suitcase – not as two women and a *métis* orphan, but as a family who knew they could be stronger together. The farm welcomed Kamia with open arms; the fields, animals and seasons bore witness to her blossoming in the ever-constant love of her two mothers.

Memories of Jacques and Ana lived on through stories and photographs, cherished and honoured as sacred relics of the past. Kamia grew tall and wise, her intellect matched only by her confidence – a beacon of what love and security could cultivate. The sisters of the local convent school accepted Kamia's exquisitely written application, inviting her for an interview. But after Kamia had spent the morning touring the grounds and classrooms, receiving a condescending welcome from most of the staff, the offer of a school place was retracted quietly and without reason. Sofia and Lina were furious although they didn't make a fuss in front of Kamia, and let the whole idea dissipate. It reeked of racism.

Undeterred, and with a stubbornness born from two mothers scorned, Lina and Sofia took it in turns to home-school Kamia in all of the same curriculum subjects, to a higher standard than any convent sister could teach.

Underneath the vast expanse of sky, amidst the chorus of nature and the rhythm of farm life interspersed with study, Kamia thrived. With every sunrise, she stood shoulder to shoulder with Sofia and Lina, her adoptive mothers, her guardians, her teachers. Together, they faced the world not just as survivors, but as equals.

The air smelled of old paper and ink as Sofia rifled through the last of the yellowed records, her eyes scanning for any trace of the name "Jacques Dumont". Beside her, Lina's fingers paused over a photograph, the edges frayed and faded, while Kamia leaned in closer, hope etched into the lines of her face.

"Nothing," Sofia murmured, the word cutting through the silence. "This is the last archive in Ostend that could have had something, anything."

The three women sat amidst a decade's worth of searching – a decade that had yielded more dead ends than answers. The once-famous bakery, which had stood as a landmark in Ostend, was now nothing but shattered bricks and lost memories, the addresses provided by Jacques during Kamia's abduction in 1939 having succumbed to the war's relentless appetite for destruction.

"Maybe it's time we accept that some trails just go cold," Lina said softly, her hand finding Kamia's, their fingers intertwining. "The war took so many great men, my love."

Kamia's gaze lingered on the photograph – a black-and-white image of a very well-presented man wearing a pressed baker's apron, his smile frozen in time. Kamia thought he looked quite "sape", like the flamboyant Congolese sapeuse. She placed it gently back on the table, resignation dulling the usual sparkle in her eyes. "Papa," she whispered, "what happened to you?"

***

Although Jacques' memory was never lost, their hope of finding out what happened to him evaporated over time.

Before they knew it, Kamia celebrated her thirtieth birthday. Like her mothers, she had been drawn to nursing, and it was no coincidence that she chose to work in the hospital, Clinique Saint-Jacques, on Rue aux Laines in the city, caring for the people of Brussels year upon year.

And so it was that in 1963 Kamia, Sofia and Lina decided that they would venture back to the Congo to trace Kamia's roots.

***

The African sun bore down unforgivingly as the three women trudged up the dirt path that led to Ana's final resting place. The Congolese village outside Léopoldville was quiet, the only sound the brush of their footsteps along the dusty road and the unmistakable call of a cuckoo. Sofia's red hair, now touched with streaks of silver, was pulled back from her face, her green eyes sharp despite the long journey in equatorial heat.

"Here," Kamia said, her voice barely above a whisper as they approached the graves. The stone markers were simple, unadorned, and yet they conveyed a story of lives interwoven with love and loss.

Lina knelt, placing a bouquet of wildflowers at the base of Ana's grave. Tears glistened in her brown eyes as she traced the engraved name with a fingertip. Sofia stood sentinel beside them, her presence a comfort, her strength an anchor in the tide of emotions that threatened to overwhelm.

It was then that Kamia noticed the second marker. "Namiri Mbala," she read aloud, the name rolling off her tongue with deep reverence. Her grandfather, a man she barely remembered, yet whose legacy coursed through her veins — buried here beside her mother.

Sofia reached out, wrapping a loving arm around one of Kamia's shoulders and resting her head on the other. There was no need for words; the gesture spoke volumes. They remained there, united not just by grief, but by the unspoken appreciation of closure — the peace that comes from acceptance and understanding.

"Wherever you are, Papa," Kamia whispered to the wind, "we haven't forgotten you."

And five more years rolled by …

The salt-tanged air whirled around them as Kamia pushed Sofia in a wheelchair along the Ostend promenade, Lina walking with the aid of a stick beside them. Although the three women all resembled Arctic explorers, wrapped up in coats, hats and a blanket for Sofia, the years of struggle and war were clearly beginning to take their toll on both mothers. The sombre sky promised rain, but for now the trio savoured the bracing touch of the autumnal wind on their exposed cheeks, each caught in a silent reverie.

"Come on," Sofia finally called out, her voice cutting through the dull roar of the waves, "let's get inside before the storm hits." She pointed a mittened hand to the cosy glow of the seaside café, its windows fogged up from the warmth within.

They hurried across the promenade, entering the café just as the first drops of rain began to spatter on the hopeful tables and chairs outside. Shaking off the cold, they settled into a corner booth, the worn red leather squeaking in protest.

"Hot chocolate all round?" Sofia suggested, her green eyes gleaming with the reflection of the café's golden light. Her hands, roughened from years of nursing, wrapped around the steaming mug the waitress brought over, the heat seeping into her skin, a comforting balm to the chill that had settled deep in her bones.

Lina nodded, eagerly wrapping her fingers around her own mug, while Kamia's eyes wandered, taking in the assorted customers who sought refuge from the impending downpour. The café hummed with hushed conversations and the odd clink of teaspoons in porcelain.

"Anything interesting?" Sofia asked, noticing Lina unfolding the local newspaper she'd picked up at the counter.

"Let's see," Lina replied, scanning the headlines. Then, without warning, the calmness shattered. "Oh!" she gasped, her hand flying to her mouth, her brown eyes wide with disbelief.

Sofia leaned forward instinctively; protective instincts honed by years of conflict stirring within her. "What is it?"

"Look!" Lina thrust the paper across the table, her finger jabbing at an article nestled among the fold. "It's him … it's Jacques!"

Sofia's gaze dropped to the print, where a black-and-white photograph of a man accompanied the text. There was no mistaking that square jaw, those piercing eyes. A hero's commendation – le Croix des Évadés – for those who escaped from the enemy and served our country valiantly in the war. And the words beneath: "Harbour master at the Royal Flandrian Yacht Club."

Kamia, who had been quietly sipping her drink, followed Sofia's gaze. The cup that slipped from her slender hands was forgotten as she looked into the face of the man she had longed to meet for more than half her life.

"Is it ... Papa?" Her voice was tremulous, a mix of hope and fear.

Without a word, Sofia nodded, her heart hammering in her chest as she watched a myriad of emotions play across Kamia's face – the culmination of years of searching, of hoping against hope.

"Go," she urged, gesturing towards the door. "We'll be right here. Go find him."

Kamia didn't need to be told twice. She was up, her athletic frame suddenly charged with an energy that seemed too vast to contain. She bolted from the café, the bell above the door jingling frantically in her wake.

Sofia and Lina exchanged a glance, a silent agreement passing between them. This was Kamia's moment; a moment that could reveal her missing jigsaw piece.

"Let's give her a head start," Sofia said, a proud smile softening her usually stern features. "Then we'll follow."

"Of course," Lina replied, her hand finding Sofia's across the table, their bond unspoken but palpable.

Outside, the rain had intensified, a steady drumbeat upon the roof of the world. But for Kamia, racing to the tram stop that would deposit her outside the Royal Flandrian Yacht Club, there was only the pounding of her heart, the pace of her stride, and the thrill of feeling complete.

Author's Note

Although much of *The Harbour Master's Secret* is fictional, it is inspired by the true wartime exploits of my friend, Pierre Leclef, (and his wife, Jenny). They had no children of their own, and their remarkable story would have been lost to the passing of time. I am one of the privileged few in this world to have had a close enough relationship that it allowed me to hear it first-hand. I wish Jenny and Pierre were still alive to tell you themselves, but this is how I came to know them, love them, and hear of their bravery, courage and strength:

Even the force of the largest waves smashing against the hull, launching the North Sea high into the air and drenching the cockpit of our small family yacht, were now so banal and monotonous that they failed to register in my awareness. My small body lurching from side to side, a fine layer of salt crusting my skin and coating every hair on my head, despite the protection of a waterproof hood. My buttocks ached and I swear they began the trip a normal round shape, but after four interminably dull hours of sitting on a hard fibreglass seat, I was convinced they'd turned square. Every inch of me was soaked and finding a more comfortable seat was futile – I was attached by a harness to the boat itself, thanks to an overly protective mother who was stubbornly and singlehandedly wrestling the sea with a steely determination that only a mum who is being tested knows. I catch a glimpse of a reassuring smile through the hood of her waterproof jacket and the sea spray. The sort of smile that says … I know, son … we'll be there soon.

This was how every summer holiday began for me and my sister. Slowly but surely the strength of our little sailing boat was winning, inching along the North European coastline to paradise. For me, a boy aged six, the destination was always worth the journey.

I longed for the people, the peace and the playground of Ostend marina. Compared to the safe rubberised tarmac and warning signs of modern playgrounds, the play area of the Royal Flandrian Yacht Club was a veritable 1980s death trap. It was meagre at best, with one dilapidated seesaw (the handle of which pinched your inner thigh skin if held too firmly) and one squeaky swing, with the fourth leg of the frame roaming free when a six-year-old was using maximum kick to reach full height. You had to approach this playground with the preparation of an Olympic gymnast – one false move and it was an injury for you. And a painful one – which was a two-person job – the strongest adult held you down whilst the other performed splinter surgery, wielding tweezers and antiseptic. As the years went by, I realised that continuing to play with a splinter embedded in a body part was preferable to telling my parents I had an injury. Upon reflection, I can confirm that the whole apparatus of the Royal Flandrian Yacht Club playground was made of rotting wood and rusty scaffolding tubes. But it was heaven to me, still with salt marks on my face and thick, wild salty hair. Even though the wonky swing was also an unforgiving seat, the aching in my backside had miraculously disappeared.

And then there were the other highlights of Belgium. Endless cartons of chocolate milkshake; the go-kart track hidden within the dense greenery of Ostend Park; a steaming bowl of fresh cooked mussels with Belgian *frites*; even the supermarket seemed exotic and adventurous. To me, Ostend was just heavenly.

The RFYC was a mile inland past the large cargo ships, the passenger ferry port, the jetfoil terminal, all the way upstream, and way past the seaside city centre. It was sheltered, a floating crossword puzzle of wooden pontoons, all connected like branches, enabling as many small motor and sailing boats to moor as possible. And by virtue of its inland position, the RFYC attracted very few visitors due to its remoteness. The moorings were overlooked by the large imposing yacht club building, with a good view straight down the harbour channel, and beyond, towards the North Sea from whence we came.

And set before the yacht club, at the top of the gangway connecting dry land with the floating pontoons, nestled the harbour master's hut.

The little circular hut was barely big enough to contain a desk and a chair, let alone a person. The varnish peeled like discarded snakeskin from the weathered timber exterior, but it was a swivel-chaired seat of power. This was the domain of Monsieur Pierre Leclef, the harbour master, a small vantage point from which all of the boats, and their comings and goings, could be monitored, and the cash-rich business of mooring fees could be conducted. It was the harbour master's job to know all the comings and goings.

As we motored excitedly towards the RFYC, our eyes were peeled keenly on the hut. Would he be there to greet us again, as he had been for as long as I could remember?

Suddenly we spied some scampering in the distance – a tiny figure, characteristic white shirt and navy trousers running down the gangway and waving frantically. Yes, it was unmistakably him!

With much smiling and shouting, Pierre directed us to an empty mooring and a joyful reunion ... speaking English in that European way – very understandable, yet requiring some concentration to decipher the correct meaning. Unmistakably European, and always welcoming, I had missed him. Within five minutes of securing our boat to the pontoon, and leaving Pierre and my parents to their grown-up chat, I had fulfilled my dream ... racing up the gangway, past Pierre's hut, and happily reacquainting myself with the playground of death.

Pierre himself always looked immaculate, even for a harbour master. Short back and sides hairstyle, Brylcreemed, with a crisp side parting. Clean white shirt with a white vest visible beneath. Black tie. Formal navy trousers. Shiny black brogues. He must have been in his sixties when I first knew him, but age did not weary him as it did others. Whilst some 63-year-olds were considering a well-earned retirement, Pierre still seemed to enjoy leaping about the moorings, shouting boat handling advice at amateurs who found themselves in bother, and catching mooring lines to help weary sailors alongside. And we had all grown very fond of him over the years.

They say that the eyes are the window to the soul. This was true for Pierre. I knew him 24 years, from age six until his death in 2004, and I was always struck by his piercing blue eyes. But you had to stop him long enough to notice. And in the quieter moments, when we had invited him down below, sat in the cabin drinking tea, he would be still, and whilst he chatted in his bubbly Belgian way to Mum and Dad, I would watch his weathered, lined face. Even though I was young there was more going on behind those eyes than anyone would know ... behind the crisp white shirt, behind the way Pierre lived quietly as a dutifully submissive husband to Jenny, behind the nimbleness and charisma ... there was something he wasn't saying ... piercing blue eyes, a little bloodshot, a little tired ... there was another world in there that he either couldn't or wouldn't share ... and the truth was that he had only ever shared it with one other person ... the only other human he had let into this other vast world. A person of such strength and safety with whom his secret could be trusted. His love, Jenny Vanslambrouck.

As the summers came and went, we became close family friends with Jenny and Pierre. Mum and Dad would stay in touch throughout the winter months, and when the ailing Pierre had finally retired as harbour master, my parents would drive to

Ostend via the Eurotunnel, retrieve the elderly but spritely couple and bring them to England to spend Christmases with us in Kent. Jenny and Pierre had not been able to conceive a family of their own, and so my sister and I became their surrogate grandchildren. As he relaxed with a cup of tea, happily observing us ripping open presents at approximately 6.42 am on Christmas morning, I recall that even Pierre's red satin paisley pyjamas were stylish. He was "sape", for sure.

But piecing together Pierre's adventures was not easy. For so many veterans, war stories are best left in the past. If you weren't there, how could you possibly understand? And what could one hope to achieve in the telling of them?

Every once in a while, Jenny would let slip a little morsel of action here and there, as the Christmases slipped by. We would beg Pierre to elaborate, and gently probe for as much as he would comfortably share. He had a trustworthy and loving audience in us, who wanted to hear it all. We simply listened in wonder, enthralled and amazed by the stories that modestly and casually unfolded. Not in one sitting, but over the years of knowing him, inch by inch. He would recall tales of his youth, catching crocs in his beloved homeland of the Belgian Congo, his resistance escapades in Bayonne, cycling hundreds of kilometres avoiding capture, the hell of imprisonment, the serendipity of narrowly missing the first resistance escape boat (which exploded four miles out to sea) and having to wait for the next. We listened, enthralled, as Pierre narrated how he took the map, and of the cinema explosion which finally pensioned him out of the navy. And we listened year after year, story by story, yearning for more.

Jenny and Pierre were like grandparents to me. We spent many summers and Christmases together. I even spent an Easter holiday living in the spare room of their flat as a very shy teenager, to practise speaking French with them before my GCSE exams. I'm now 50 years old, and in 2023, Jenny passed away, having survived without her soulmate, Pierre, for 19 years. Whilst Pierre was happy with quiet subservience, Jenny was a force of nature – larger than life, also immaculately dressed, always in full cosmetic make-up (except at 6.42 am on Christmas morning) and demanding to a fault. Her work colleagues might have referred to her as a bit of a tyrant, but not me – to me she was kind, to me she was family.

I miss them both, dearly.

And with that, I have achieved my mission – to remember Jenny and Pierre, and to pass a story inspired by them, on to you.

Author Profile

Simon Thomas spends his time based on carefully chosen priorities, chiefly as dad to his sons, Ollie and Jack, and husband to Suzie. He enjoys keeping active in the great outdoors of the Yorkshire Dales, and is devoted to his cockapoo, Poppy. After discovering his vocation in 2014, Simon travels far and wide creating interactive and engaging training experiences for individuals and teams, to build people skills through learning.

***

What Did You Think of *The Harbour Master's Secret?*

A big thank you for purchasing this book. It means a lot that you chose this book specifically from such a wide range on offer. I do hope you enjoyed it.

Book reviews are incredibly important for an author. All feedback helps them improve their writing for future projects and for developing this edition. If you are able to spare a few minutes to post a review on Amazon, that would be much appreciated.

Publisher Information

Rowanvale Books provides publishing services to independent authors, writers and poets all over the globe. We deliver a personal, honest and efficient service that allows authors to see their work published, while remaining in control of the process and retaining their creativity. By making publishing services available to authors in a cost-effective and ethical way, we at Rowanvale Books hope to ensure that the local, national and international community benefits from a steady stream of good quality literature.

For more information about us, our authors or our publications, please get in touch.

www.rowanvalebooks.com
info@rowanvalebooks.com

Printed in Great Britain
by Amazon

61615110R00120